# DANGEROUS RELATIONS

## CAROL J. POST

W9-AUK-389

Recycling programs
for this product may
not exist in your area.

LOVE INSPIRED BOOKS

ISBN-13: 978-1-335-67918-5

Dangerous Relations

www.Harlequin.com

**Printed in U.S.A.**

The Lord is nigh unto all them that call upon him...
—*Psalms* 145:18

Thanks to my friend Nicole Little,
who showed me around North Bend and Snoqualmie
and patiently answered a gazillion questions.

Thanks to my son-in-law Mike Daunis,
who helped me with all things navy.
(Thank you for your twenty years of service.)

Thanks to my sister Kimberly Wolff,
who not only plots with me but has a built-in radar and
works hard to keep this directionally challenged author
straight. You're the best sis ever!

Thank you to my editor, Dina Davis, and my
critique partners, Karen Fleming and Sabrina Jarema,
for making my stories the best they can be.

And thank you to my husband, Chris, for encouragement,
computer help, brainstorming and buying me chocolate.

## "Someone was here." Ryan nodded toward the door.

Shelby shifted Chloe to one hip and looked. A breeze lifted a sheet of paper that was affixed to the door. Her chest tightened as a sense of vulnerability swept through her. She scanned the area. No one was loitering nearby. Unless someone was watching them from the woods.

When she glanced back at Ryan, tension emanated from him. He was wearing a light windbreaker-type jacket. Did he have his weapon underneath?

"Let's get inside." He nodded toward the door.

She stepped onto the landing and jammed the key into the lock. Ryan waited until she and Chloe were safely inside before he followed them in.

"Call the police."

Shelby tensed at the urgency in his tone. "What does it say?"

"Paraphrasing? He's watching."

Shelby began to pace. "What's that telling us that we don't already know? Addy has seen him twice. You chased him."

"There's more. He said someday there'll be no one here to protect you." Ryan's jaw tightened. "And Chloe might become collateral damage."

**Carol J. Post** writes fun and fast-paced inspirational romantic suspense stories and lives in sunshiny central Florida. She sings and plays the piano for her church and also enjoys sailing, hiking and camping—almost anything outdoors. Her daughters and grandkids live too far away for her liking, so she now pours all that nurturing into taking care of two fat and sassy cats and one highly spoiled dachshund.

## Books by Carol J. Post

### Love Inspired Suspense

# ONE

Shelby Adair cruised down I-90, trying to drum up some enthusiasm for the evening ahead. No matter how she pitched it, she couldn't find many bright spots in the prospect of spending two or three hours with her self-absorbed sister.

But Mia's company wasn't the reason she'd scheduled the dinner date. She was an aunt. And she was going to be a good one.

She cast a glance over her shoulder and moved into the far-left lane. Soon she'd cross Lake Washington and join the other vehicles that made up Seattle's rush-hour traffic. But during the late afternoon, coming in wasn't as bad as going out. Barring the unexpected, she should arrive at Mia's apartment complex in thirty minutes.

She was seeing her sister twice in one month. That was a record. But she'd had a valid reason for avoiding contact. Between caring for their dying aunt and keeping the diner afloat, she'd had a full plate. Dealing with Mia's theatrics would have sent her over the edge.

Now that her aunt was gone, she had no excuse. Besides, she did want to connect with her fifteen-month-old niece. And with her dysfunctional childhood nine years behind her, she might have a shot at developing a relationship with one of her siblings.

It wouldn't happen with her older sister. Lauren had escaped at eighteen, moved to the other side of the country and never looked back. She hadn't even responded to Shelby's voice mails and Facebook messages about their aunt. She hadn't come to the funeral, either.

Ten minutes later, brake lights lit up the road, and Shelby slowed to a crawl. This was one reason she was glad she'd left Seattle for the sleepy, picturesque town of North Bend. It was only thirty miles away but had always felt like a small chunk of paradise.

She finally exited the interstate and negotiated her Lincoln Town Car through a series of turns. Mia's apartment complex was ahead on the right. Red and blue lights strobed through trees still bare from winter.

As she moved closer, the muscles drew tight across her shoulders. Two Seattle police cruisers and a crime-scene unit sat in front of the building that housed Mia's apartment.

Her sister's words echoed in her thoughts, fragments of a conversation they'd had after the funeral. Mia had said there was something going on at the club where she worked, that if she stumbled across exactly what it was, her life would be in danger. Shelby hadn't taken her seriously at the time.

She still didn't. Mia was the ultimate drama queen, the proverbial "girl who cried wolf." Anything for attention. She'd been crafting fantastic stories since she was old enough to talk.

Shelby stopped in a visitor parking space and killed the engine. When she reached for the door handle, the lights strobing in her side mirror sent tension through her again.

She tried to shake it off. This was a three-story apartment complex. There were more than thirty units in Mia's building alone. The probability that the police vehicles had anything to do with Mia or little Chloe was low.

She stepped into the chilly March air as a Toyota Prius approached. When it passed, her gaze locked onto the back and stuck. Large black letters stretched across the white rear bumper— Medical Examiner. Parked three spaces down was a white van with the same designation.

Her breath hitched and something dark settled over her. The presence of the medical examiner meant one thing.

Someone was dead.

While the Prius parked, she sprinted toward the building, heart pounding in her chest. It couldn't be Mia. What her sister had said at Aunt Bea's funeral was an attention-getting ploy, just like all the other times. Having grown up with Mia, Shelby had her number. Letting the tales get to her was never a good idea.

She bypassed the elevator and ran up the steps, taking them two at a time. She'd never been to her sister's apartment, but Mia had given her the number—312.

When Shelby burst into the third-floor hallway, a vise clamped down on her chest. Two apartments away, the door was ajar. A woman stood in front of the opening, soothing a crying child in her arms. Tears had left streaks in the woman's makeup. She wasn't familiar. The child was.

Where was Mia? Why was Chloe being held by a crying stranger?

Shelby rushed forward, then skidded to a stop. The gold numbers affixed to the metal door put to death the irrational hope that the apartment belonged to someone else. The woman shifted Chloe to her other hip, and Shelby peered around her.

Beyond the entry, a crime-scene tech was

kneeling with her back to the door. Next to her, a red smear marked the beige tiles.

Shelby's stomach did a free fall, and her knees threatened to buckle. Maybe that wasn't Mia's blood on the floor. A friend lived with her and helped care for Chloe. Addy, if she remembered correctly.

She shifted her gaze to the woman and spoke over the little girl's cries. "I'm Shelby, Mia's sister. What's going on?"

The woman's gaze met hers. "It's Mia."

"What's Mia? What happened?"

"She's gone."

"Gone where?"

The woman squeezed her eyes shut and shook her head. "Gone."

Shelby's mind spun, searching all the possible interpretations of "gone." Mia could be gone on an errand. But that wouldn't explain the woman's tears. Maybe Mia had decided she couldn't cope with the pressures of motherhood and disappeared, deserting her little girl.

That was the explanation Shelby clung to, because the most obvious one was unthinkable. Her twenty-one-year-old sister couldn't be dead.

"I went to the store." The woman's tone was flat. "I took Chloe with me, so Mia could take a nap. When I got back, Mia was…" A shudder shook her shoulders. "She was on the floor in front of the couch. Someone had slit her throat."

"Is she…?" The final word wouldn't come out.

At the woman's nod, Shelby collapsed against the doorjamb and sank to the floor. Mia was dead. Shelby had finally decided to mend their relationship, but it was too late.

And Chloe was orphaned. Her playboy daddy wouldn't step up. Based on what Mia had said after the funeral, the guy was worthless.

So it all fell on Shelby. The realization knocked the last of the wind from her.

She was no stranger to responsibility. Through her adolescent and teen years, she'd pretty much raised Mia. They hadn't been orphans, at least not in the traditional sense. But with a father who worked long hours, an older sister who took off the moment she became an adult and a mother who had years earlier retreated to her room and withdrawn from life, managing the Adair household became Shelby's responsibility.

At eighteen, she'd traded one mantle for another, taking care of Aunt Bea through grueling rounds of chemo and radiation while keeping the diner afloat. At twenty-five, she'd done it again when the cancer returned. That stint had lasted two years, ending with her aunt's death two weeks ago.

But this was different. She had no clue how to raise a child. The way Mia had turned out was proof.

She pushed herself to her feet and straightened her shoulders. She hadn't known how to run a diner, either, but she'd figured it out.

She held out her hands, palms up. "Come to Aunt Shelby, sweetie."

Chloe wrapped her arms more tightly around the woman's neck. When Shelby tried to take her, the child released an ear-piercing wail.

"She's not used to you." The woman's tone seemed to hold a note of accusation. Or maybe that was Shelby's own guilt.

"I've been…" What, busy? Too busy to be a part of her niece's life when she lived forty-five minutes away?

The woman rubbed Chloe's back in slow circles, whispering soothing words. The screams quieted to gut-wrenching sobs.

Shelby crossed her arms. "Are you Chloe's babysitter?"

"Nanny." She extended her right hand. "Addy Sorenson."

Shelby shook the woman's hand. Addy wasn't what she'd pictured. Nannies didn't normally wear skin-hugging jeans and sweaters with plunging necklines. Add the brilliant blue eyes and the thick mane of hair flowing down her back like black silk, and she couldn't be further from the stereotypical image of a nanny.

Of course, Mia hadn't gotten her from a nanny-for-hire ad. Right after Chloe was born, Shelby had visited Mia in the hospital. Mia had planned to go back to her bartender job at the club and had arranged child care—a former coworker named Addy. She'd had a hysterectomy and never returned to work. Apparently, the woman loved children so much she agreed to provide full-time care for little more than room and board. So Mia had gotten a live-in nanny on a day-care budget.

Shelby didn't know what Addy's job at the club had been. It didn't matter. If she'd been caring for Chloe the past fifteen months, she had to know what she was doing. Having her around would also provide some stability in the little girl's life.

A short distance away, the elevator dinged and two men stepped off. One was a couple of decades older than her and was carrying a black case—he was likely from the medical examiner's office. The occupant of the white van was apparently inside already. The man nodded at her and Addy, then disappeared into the apartment.

When the other one approached, Chloe twisted and reached for him. "Wyan."

*Wyan?*

Addy altered her grip to better hold the now squirming child. "Ryan." Her tone was tight. Maybe there was some history between them.

As soon as he took Chloe from her, the child's arms went around his neck and she pressed her face against his throat. "Wyan." The cries faded to shuddering breaths.

*Ryan.* Shelby frowned. Chloe's father's name was Randall. So who was Ryan? And why was the little girl clinging to him when she wouldn't let Shelby touch her?

Shelby studied the man holding her niece. He was younger than the one who'd just stepped into the apartment, probably in his mid-to-late thirties. He obviously didn't spend all his time behind a desk. His black T-shirt stretched taut across a well-defined chest, and as he held Chloe in his arms, his pose showed off impressive biceps. Clean-shaven with a buzz cut, he had the air of a military guy. Or maybe a cop.

He leveled serious brown eyes on Addy. "What's going on?"

"Mia's dead."

His jaw dropped. "What? How?"

"Murdered. Throat slashed."

The blood drained from his face and he

sagged against the wall. His arms tightened around the child he held. "Has a decision been made about Chloe?"

"Not yet. The cops just took my statement. They told me not to go anywhere."

He swallowed hard, his throat working with the action. "If they'll allow it, she can come home with me until I can get legal custody."

"Whoa, wait a minute." Shelby held up both hands, trying to stop the runaway train she was trapped on. She'd just lost her sister. She wasn't about to let a stranger walk away with her niece. "Who are you?"

His gaze swept her face. "I'm her uncle."

The pieces were falling into place, but she didn't like where they were landing. "Randall's brother."

A tightness flitted across his features, but was gone so quickly, she might have imagined it. He nodded then returned his attention to Addy. "It'll be a while before they let us inside. I'll go buy whatever Chloe might need for the next day or two."

Shelby dropped her hands, curling them into fists. Randall wasn't just Chloe's good-for-nothing daddy. He also managed his father's club, where Mia had worked. She'd said something shady was going on there, something that had made her fear for her life. Whatever Ryan's involvement in his family's businesses, Shelby wasn't about to send Chloe home with him.

"I know what Mia would want." Though soft, Addy's words jarred her. "I was there when Chloe was born. I'm her godmother. Mia intended for me to raise her if anything happened."

Shelby frowned. "A godmother isn't a legal guardian."

The handsome stranger lifted a brow. "And you are?"

"Shelby Adair. I'm Chloe's aunt, Mia's sister."

"Ah." His tone seemed to hold a lot of meaning. What was he getting at?

He nodded. "I can see the resemblance."

She narrowed her eyes. He was trying to soften her so she'd let him take Chloe. But she was no pushover. And she wasn't swayed by empty flattery.

Mia was beautiful. Shelby had heard it all her life—Lauren was the smart one and Mia was the pretty one. Apparently, Shelby was neither.

That was okay. What she lacked in beauty and brains, she'd always made up for in ambition. And determination.

She planted her hands on her hips. "Chloe's going home with me."

If Ryan McConnell thought otherwise, he was in for a fight.

\* \* \*

Ryan tamped down the annoyance building inside him. As soon as the Navy had assigned him to Naval Base Kitsap, across the bay from his hometown of Seattle, he'd started prodding his brother to do the right thing. Mia had been six months pregnant then.

By the time Chloe was born, he'd given up. His younger brother never dealt with the consequences of his actions, so Ryan had resolved to be a fixture in his niece's life from day one.

That was more than he could say for the woman in front of him.

"You're Chloe's aunt. Where do you live?"

"North Bend."

"That close. As often as I'm here, our paths should have crossed."

The determination on her face seemed to waver. He knew exactly who Shelby was. Mia had told him about her siblings, both of whom had pretty much severed ties with their younger sister. Now that Mia was gone, one of those sisters was on her doorstep, ready to take away his niece. Not in this lifetime.

He pressed a kiss to the top of Chloe's head. "Let's be frank. When was the last time you saw your niece?"

She lifted her chin. "Two weeks ago."

"Your aunt's funeral." Mia had told him about that, too. "Before that?"

She looked away briefly, then jerked her gaze back to his. Keeping her eyes fixed on him seemed to require some effort. "That's irrelevant."

"I'd say it's quite relevant. Chloe just lost her mother." She might have even witnessed the murder.

He glanced at Addy, but she was staring past him, down the hall. The muscles in the side of her face tensed. She probably felt the same way about Chloe's absentee aunt as he did. She brushed past him and mumbled, "Excuse me," then stalked down the hall. At the end, she pulled open the door to the stairs and let it swing closed behind her.

Since he had Chloe, she was probably taking advantage of her first opportunity to be alone. She had to be reeling. He certainly was.

When he drew his gaze back to Shelby, she stood with her arms crossed. The determination was back full force. "Chloe needs care and love. Those are things I can provide."

"She needs to be surrounded by people she knows, not taken away by a virtual stranger."

She pursed her lips. At first glance, she was a toned-down, natural version of Mia. They had the same slope to their jaws and the same high cheekbones. Shelby's shoulder-length hair was the same deep auburn shade as her sister's, at least when Mia wasn't wearing one of the multitude of wigs that were part of her showgirl persona.

But the similarities ended there. First was the age spread. Mia had said there were six-year spans between the three sisters. As the middle child, Shelby would be twenty-seven.

Next was their makeup. Mia dolled herself up almost as much for a trip to the grocery store as a shift at the club. If Shelby was wearing cosmetics at all, they were understated.

The biggest difference was in their eyes. Though the same golden green as Mia's, Shelby's held seriousness in their depths, even wisdom, as if her life experience exceeded her age. As if she'd been forced to grow up too quickly.

He sighed. "Why are you here?"

"Mia and Chloe and I had dinner plans."

He lifted an eyebrow. He was supposed to believe that? "Dinner plans. Tonight."

"Yes."

"Why? You've hardly said boo to Mia since you left home."

She narrowed her eyes. "My relationship with my sister isn't the issue. All that matters is doing what's best for her little girl."

At least they agreed on something. "And that's staying with me."

She heaved a sigh. "Since we're being frank, let me lay it out. I own a diner. I live in a small town where neighbors still say 'hi' to one another. My living quarters are upstairs from where I work. I can pop in anytime to check on Chloe. I'll hire a good babysitter—preferably Addy, if she's willing."

Yeah, she'd be willing. She was crazy about Chloe. And Chloe was just as attached to her. Regardless of how Addy felt about him, her presence was good for Chloe. So Ryan would make sure she stayed on once he got custody. And he *was* going to get custody, whatever it took.

Shelby continued, "I'm not wealthy, but I can provide a good, wholesome environment. Besides the love I'll give her, she'll have the influences of my aunt's church and our friends."

"I can provide the same thing." He'd even consider church attendance for Chloe's sake.

Shelby lifted one arched brow. "Your family owns a bunch of gentlemen's clubs. That's hardly the environment for a little girl to grow up in."

He clenched his teeth. The woman was judging him for his father's activities after she'd had nothing to do with Chloe because she was too busy or too snooty or just plain didn't care.

When he spoke, ice edged his tone. "I'm not my family." At least not his father's side. Instead, he'd been closer to his mother, especially after his parents divorced when he was seven. At age twelve, he'd found a father figure through his best friend. A recently retired military man, Kyle's dad had adored his wife and made his children the center of his life. Ryan's ideals had been on an increasingly separate path from his father's ever since.

A detective holding a small notepad approached from inside the apartment. He glanced at them both, then focused on Ryan. "What is your relationship with Mia Adair?"

"I'm the baby's uncle. My brother is the father." At the detective's request, he provided his contact information.

"How often did you see Mia?"

"Three or four times a week."

"Where?"

"Here. I'd pick up Chloe and take her to the park and places." He'd call Mia and let her know he was on the way. She was always fine with it. Except today she hadn't answered. Since he'd already been in Seattle on another errand, he figured he'd give it a shot.

"Have you and Ms. Adair ever dated?"

"We've never been more than friends." If not for Chloe, she wouldn't have even been that. She was too shallow to be someone with whom he'd seek out a friendship.

"Do you know of anyone who would want to hurt her?"

"No. I didn't think she had enemies. She seemed to get along with everybody."

At the end of the hall, the elevator dinged and the doors opened. Addy stepped off and approached. The detective gave her a brief glance, then continued his questions. Once finished, he turned to Shelby.

"What about you? What is your relationship with Ms. Adair?"

"Her sister."

While he jotted her name, address and phone number in his pad, Ryan smoothed Chloe's curls, so soft against his palm. She lifted her eyes to his. They were green with gold flecks, just like her mother's. Like her aunt's, too.

"Are you aware of anyone who'd have wanted to hurt her?"

Ryan watched Shelby's gaze shift to him before going back to the detective. Uneasiness brushed the edges of his mind.

"Yes."

"Who?"

"The people who own and manage the club where she worked."

Ryan's jaw dropped. "Come on." The objection slipped out before he could stop it. The woman would resort to anything to get Chloe.

The detective shot him a warning glance. "What club is that?"

"The Satin Cabaret."

"Why do you believe her employers would want to hurt her?"

"She told me there was something shady going on at the club. She'd seen or heard something. She said if she stumbled on what it was, her life would be in danger."

"When did she tell you this?"

"Two weeks ago."

"Did she say what she'd seen or heard?"

"No."

"Could she have been talking about patrons rather than the owners?"

"Possibly, but that wasn't the impression I got. Since she said something shady was going on at the club, I assume it's something the owners are involved in. Or know about, anyway."

He finished his notes, then looked up. "Anything else you can tell me?"

"Not that I remember."

"Call if you think of anything." He handed

each of them a card with a case number. "Will one of you be taking the child, or shall I call DSHS?"

Shelby jumped in. "I'm taking her." She looked at Addy. "Will you continue as Chloe's nanny?"

Addy nodded. "I go wherever Chloe goes."

"Good." Shelby returned her attention to the detective. "I'll file the necessary paperwork to make it legal. Based on what Mia told me, Chloe's daddy is out of the picture. I'm expecting him to sign away his parental rights."

Ryan held up a hand. "With all due respect, even though Ms. Adair is Chloe's aunt, Chloe has seen her only a handful of times. She needs to be with people she knows, people who love her."

Fire lit Shelby's eyes. He wasn't accusing her of not loving Chloe. But based on the glare he was getting, that was how she'd taken it. "His brother manages the club where my sister worked. His father owns it. These are the people my sister was afraid of."

"According to you."

Addy frowned. "Mia told me the same thing."

"That has nothing to do with me." Ryan struggled to keep his voice level. "I'm almost finished with twenty years in the Navy. I've never been involved in my family's business."

Shelby spread her arms, palms up. "We don't

even know that Randall McConnell's name is on Chloe's birth certificate. According to Mia, they've never been in a committed relationship."

The detective closed his pad. "Until the courts can sort it out, it makes sense for the child to go with the deceased's sister."

Ryan sagged against the hallway wall. How was this happening? After he'd spent countless hours bonding with his niece, how could Chloe's absentee aunt walk in and lay claim to her?

He'd let it go tonight. He'd lost the initial battle, but not the war. Shelby had said she was filing the necessary paperwork. He would, too. He'd fight her every step of the way.

His brother wasn't going to be any help. The idiot had gotten himself arrested a week ago. It wasn't the first time. He'd been able to beat the other charges or accept pleas for reduced sentences. Ryan had warned him—one more time and they'd put him *under* the jail. Randall hadn't listened. This time he'd sold heroin to an undercover cop. He probably wouldn't see freedom for the next fifteen years. Or longer.

This weekend, Ryan would visit and tell him about Mia. There wouldn't be tears. Men didn't cry, especially McConnell men. At least, that was what he and Randall had been taught from a young age. Over the past twenty years, Ryan had learned his father was wrong. Sometimes men *did* cry, even McConnell men.

He turned to Shelby. "Can we exchange phone numbers?" He kept the irritation from his tone. Alienating her further wouldn't do them any good. "I'd like to stay in touch with my niece. I'll also try to answer any questions you might have."

After some hesitation, she removed her phone from her purse. "Give me your number."

As he rattled off the digits, her thumbs flew over her screen. Moments later, his phone buzzed with an incoming text. Time to hand over his niece. He buried his face in her curly copper-colored hair. The faint scent of her shampoo, a combination of strawberries and bananas, wrapped around him. He kissed her again, then tried to untangle her arms from his neck. She tightened her hold.

"Sweetie, you need to go with Aunt Shelby." The words tasted bitter. Shelby didn't deserve that title.

Chloe's eyes filled with tears. "No. Wyan."

He injected false cheer into his voice. "Uncle Ryan will see you soon." It was a promise he hoped he could keep.

Chloe began to cry in earnest. As he transferred her into Shelby's waiting arms, the cries became full-blown wails.

His eyes met Shelby's. Then he turned and strode toward the elevator. Chloe's cries followed him, each one shredding his heart.

When he stepped outside, the lingering remnants of daylight had faded to night. He slid into his Equinox and let his head fall back against the seat. In a few minutes, a stranger would walk away with his niece. She'd never be what Chloe needed. When she couldn't even be bothered to make an occasional visit, how would she make the sacrifices needed to raise an emotionally healthy child?

She wouldn't.

He heaved a sigh. He should head back to his apartment, but he couldn't bring himself to leave. Maybe he wanted to catch one more glimpse of his niece before Shelby took her away. Or if he sat there long enough, maybe he'd somehow make sense of the whole messed-up situation.

Addy walked from the building carrying Chloe. Shelby followed behind. She'd already passed off her parenting responsibility. He wasn't surprised.

They walked to Addy's Camaro, where Addy fastened Chloe into her car seat in the back. After a short exchange, Shelby walked toward her own vehicle. Her head was down, her shoulders slumped. Sadness wrapped around her like a cloak.

An unwelcome sense of compassion stirred inside him. He wanted to hate her, to view her as the enemy. But that picture wasn't right. Because upstairs, in that final moment before he'd turned away, her eyes hadn't held triumph. They'd held pain.

He reached for his keys, which were hanging in the ignition. Behind him, a vehicle roared down the short road that ran past the apartment complex. Someone was blowing right through the posted 25-mile-per-hour speed limit. As he turned the key, Shelby cast a sudden glance back at Addy. His own engine rumbled to life, blending with the roar of the other one. But there was something else, too—a pop, the sharp crack of a vehicle backfiring.

Or a gunshot.

A short distance away, Shelby dove between two cars. Ryan sprang from his vehicle at the same time Addy slipped into the Camaro and slammed the door behind her.

Now he had no doubt. What he'd heard was a gunshot. Had it come from the vehicle that had just sped past?

He dialed 911, then ran toward Addy's car. First, he'd see to his niece's safety. Then he'd check on Shelby. The dispatcher came on as he reached the Camaro. Addy was twisted sideways, her upper body lying over the console. Chloe was watching him from her car seat, apparently oblivious.

He spoke into the phone as he swung open the driver door. "There was a shot fired. A drive-by." That was his assumption, anyway. Addy straightened, her eyes wide, and he lifted a brow at her. She nodded.

"What kind of vehicle?" He repeated to Addy the question he'd been asked.

"Four-door. Older. I don't know what kind. It's too dark."

Shelby approached and stopped to stand next to him. He didn't take time to acknowledge her presence.

"Color?"

"Dark. Maybe. It's hard to tell."

After he relayed the information to the dispatcher, he looked at Shelby. "Did you see anything?"

She shook her head. "I heard the engine rev, but when Addy screamed that someone had a gun, I dove for cover."

He confirmed their location, then ended the call. The authorities investigating Mia's murder were still there. So were the people from the medical examiner's office. But other units would arrive shortly. In the meantime, everyone in the area would be alerted to be on the lookout for an older four-door…something. He heaved a sigh. They didn't have much to go on.

Shelby crossed her arms in front of her, then ran her hands up and down her jacket sleeves. The temperature had dropped since the sun went down. A shudder ripped through her. "Why?"

Addy lifted one shoulder, then let it fall. "Whoever killed Mia probably thinks you know something."

"But I don't."

"*I* know that. But they apparently don't, because when I saw the arm come out the window, that gun was pointed at you."

The last of the color drained from her face, and she started to teeter sideways.

Ryan grabbed her arm to steady her. "Whoa, easy."

She tilted her head back, locking those gold-green eyes on him. The vulnerability he saw there punched him in the gut.

She'd neglected her niece, ignored her sister and fought him for Chloe.

But there was no way he'd leave her at the mercy of a ruthless killer.

# TWO

Shelby pulled into a parking space at Safeway and killed the engine. The wiper blades came to a stop, forming two diagonal lines across her windshield. Outside, the usual Seattle-area drizzle fell from gray skies.

She reached for the door handle and drew her jacket's hood over her head. A folded umbrella lay on the back passenger floorboard. Other than a few times when she'd held it over Aunt Bea's head while walking her into the doctor's office, Shelby couldn't remember when she'd last opened it. Sporting an umbrella was a sure way to look like a tourist. Anyone who'd lived in the Pacific Northwest for long was used to the weeping clouds and had invested in at least one good rain jacket.

Before stepping from the Town Car, she scanned the area. She'd done the same thing driving in but hadn't seen any threats. She didn't see any now, either. No one lurking. No older, four-door cars.

She stepped from her vehicle and walked toward the store. She'd closed the diner at three. By the time she and her small staff had everything cleaned and prepped for tomorrow, it had been four. Now she was beat.

Last night had been rough. Every time she'd fallen into a sound sleep, she'd been jolted awake as one shock wave after another rippled through her. Mia was gone. It still didn't seem possible.

She walked through the automatic glass doors and snagged a shopping cart. She'd made a list at lunchtime. Fortunately, the detectives had allowed Addy and her to go in and gather some belongings before they'd headed back to North Bend.

Chloe's sleep seemed to have been as fitful as hers. Several times during the night, she'd awoken crying for her mother. Shelby's heart had twisted with every pathetic plea. One part of her wanted to keep Mia's memory alive. Another part hoped Chloe would forget quickly. When the memory faded, so would the pain.

Her ringtone sounded from her purse. She brought the cart to a halt and scrambled for her phone, her pulse in overdrive. Once she settled into the role of motherhood, maybe she wouldn't fear that every call was an emergency, a problem with Chloe.

It wasn't that she had her doubts about Addy as a caretaker. In fact, Addy hadn't called once all day. And all four times Shelby had slipped upstairs to check on them, Addy had had everything under control.

Instead of Addy, Ryan McConnell showed up on her phone's ID. After she'd gotten home last night, she'd pulled up the text she'd sent him and saved his information in her contacts.

She swiped the screen and said a curt hello.

"Hi, Shelby. It's Ryan."

He had a nice voice, rich and smooth. She hadn't noticed last night. At first, she'd been too busy dodging his accusations and trying to keep him from taking her niece. Then she'd been too shaken about almost being shot. She still didn't know whether it was a random drive-by shooting or if someone was targeting her. If the latter, the shooter hadn't followed her away from Seattle. Ryan had made sure of that. He'd insisted on escorting them all the way to North Bend.

"How is Chloe?"

"Fine. Addy said she did well today, all things considered. I checked on her several times, too." She wished she could say Chloe was starting to warm up to her, but she didn't seem to want anyone except Addy.

"I'm glad to hear that. I'm off duty now and would love to stop by and see her, if that's okay."

*Great.* She hoped he wasn't planning to have daily contact. Adjusting to motherhood was stressful enough without having critical eyes on her.

But after seeing them together yesterday evening, how could she refuse him contact with his niece? His love was almost palpable. Chloe obviously adored him, too.

She sighed. "I just arrived at the grocery store. Give me an hour."

"I'll see you in an hour and a half."

She ended the call and dropped her phone back into her purse. Once she arrived home, she'd work on dinner and let Addy entertain their guest.

Actually, he didn't need entertainment. He was there to play with his niece. But Shelby would have to invite him to stay for dinner. She couldn't send a single guy away at mealtime without feeding him.

She assumed he was single, anyway. But she hadn't looked for a wedding ring. Frankly, it didn't matter. Maybe he was a nice guy under normal circumstances. She just hadn't gotten to experience the relaxed, cordial side of him.

Whatever happened between them, they'd eventually have to settle into some kind of a mutual understanding. Like an annoying ex forever in her life because of a child between them, Ryan McConnell wasn't going away.

Thirty minutes later, she hurried to her Town Car and loaded her groceries into the trunk. The silver Lincoln didn't exactly say "single young lady," but it had originally belonged to Aunt Bea. Although almost a decade old, it was in pristine condition. When her aunt had become too sick to drive, it had made more sense for Shelby to sell her high-mileage Corolla and keep the little-used Town Car.

Before reaching the building that housed the diner on North Bend Way, Shelby took a left, then turned into the alley that ran along the back. Addy's Camaro was parked in one of the angled spaces opposite the stairs leading to the diner. Shelby pulled in next to her.

As she climbed from the car, a sense of uneasiness swept through her. She'd never given the seclusion a second thought. Now, hemmed in by the building on one side and railroad tracks and woods on the other, she felt suddenly vulnerable.

After retrieving her groceries from the trunk, she made her way up the wooden stairs, two plastic bags looped over each arm. When the diner was open, she used the interior stairwell off one side of the kitchen. After hours, the exterior entrance was more convenient.

She stepped under the awning covering the top landing and inserted her key. When she swung open the door, an older couple sat on the couch, Chloe in the woman's lap. Addy occupied the love seat. All eyes went to Shelby, and conversation ceased. Whoever Addy's guests were, they'd apparently parked in front or around the side of the building.

The woman spoke first. "You must be Mia's sister."

Shelby pushed the door shut with one hip. "I am. If you'll give me a minute, I'll be right with you."

After plopping the bags on the kitchen counter, she fished through them and pulled out the perishables. Ice cream was her one guilty pleasure, and she wasn't going to leave it melting on the counter.

When she'd finished with the cold items, she stopped at the hall tree next to the door and shed her coat, claiming the last of the four curved wooden hooks. Then she sat next to Addy and waited for someone to begin.

The woman wrapped one of Chloe's hands in hers. "We're Robert and Dorothy McConnell, Chloe's grandparents."

Shelby nodded. She'd expected as much. They

both had that aura about them, the air that said their world spun on a different axis and only intersected with those of the common people when necessary. Robert McConnell's suit obviously didn't come from a discount store. Neither did his leather loafers. His wife was classic elegance in a charcoal pencil skirt and long-sleeved silk blouse. A Louis Vuitton handbag sat next to her.

Mrs. McConnell's chin lifted, amplifying that air of superiority. "Chloe has spent a lot of time at our estate. She's bonded with us. She has her own suite, a nanny, a complete wardrobe and every toy imaginable. She'll go to the best private schools and have everything she could want or need. You could still come for visits when you can find the time."

Shelby curled her fingers into her palms as fire flared inside. *When you can find the time.* They were looking down their proud noses at her, the same way Ryan had. In fact, Ryan had probably sent them to try to coerce her into giving his family, and ultimately him, custody.

It wouldn't work.

"I'm going to raise Chloe. I spoke with a lawyer this morning who is preparing the paperwork."

Mr. McConnell released a humorless laugh. "Don't be ridiculous. What does a single woman with a diner to run want with raising someone else's child?"

"That child is my niece."

Mrs. McConnell pulled Chloe against her. "And she's our grandchild."

"Why would you want to be tied down with a little one at your ages?" Shelby had no idea what those ages might be. Ryan's dad had a little bit of middle-age spread but was still in decent shape. Based on the fine wrinkles around his eyes and mouth and the amount of gray in his hair, she would put him in his early-to-mid sixties.

His mom's age was anybody's guess. Smooth skin stretched taut over high cheekbones. Every trace of frown lines and crow's-feet had been erased, likely before they'd had a chance to fully form. She'd had work done, probably more than once.

The woman straightened her spine, and her eyes flashed with indignation. "Because we love her and want what's best for her."

"What's best for children doesn't always involve money." She'd already had this conversation with Ryan. Since he'd likely relayed every detail, there was no need to rehash it.

Mr. McConnell pushed himself to his feet. Now standing, he towered over her. "You're going to regret this."

His words had a hard edge. His gaze held the same haughtiness his wife's had. But there was something else, something cold and cruel. A chill passed through her.

She straightened her shoulders and stood. If she was going to let Ryan or his father intimidate her, she should just hand over Chloe now. "Are you threatening me?"

He stepped closer, and she willed her feet to remain planted. He had her five-foot-seven height beat by a good six inches. But it wasn't his size that made her long to retreat. His presence filled the room, and power radiated from him, brutal and deadly.

His eyes narrowed. "Just giving sound advice. Don't engage in battles you can't win."

"I'm Chloe's aunt. Your son's name isn't even on the birth certificate." She hadn't seen it, but she'd discussed it with Addy last night. Apparently, it was tucked into the folder of important papers in the bottom of Mia's two-drawer file cabinet.

"Doesn't matter." Confidence underlined the words. "A simple paternity test will show that she's our granddaughter."

"I don't need a paternity test to prove she's my niece."

"You don't. But I doubt you have deep enough pockets to go up against one of the most powerful families in Seattle. You'll have every bit of the equity in this little diner encumbered before you get to first base."

"We'll see."

His gaze shifted to his wife. "Come on, Dorothy, let's go."

As she handed Chloe to Addy, Mrs. McConnell pressed her lips together, her jaw tight. Was it determination? Or did she disapprove of her husband's strong-arm tactics?

Ryan's father dragged her to her feet, then stalked toward the door, pulling her with him. His gait held more purpose than anger. After grabbing their coats and ushering his wife through the open door, he cast Shelby a final glance. "You're willing to risk your diner. What about your life?"

Moments later, the door shut with a solid thud. Shelby rushed forward to throw the dead bolt, then stood with both hands on the wall, calming her churning thoughts.

"You did the right thing."

Shelby spun and lifted a hand to her chest, her heart pounding beneath her palm. Addy stood in front of her, still holding Chloe. Shelby hadn't heard her rise, let alone cross the room.

Addy's gaze dipped. "You're shaking."

Yeah, she was shaking. She'd had her life threatened twice over the course of twenty-four hours. But fear wasn't all she had tumbling through her. If she never saw a McConnell again, life would be good. When Ryan had been unable to use his relationship with Chloe to sway her, he'd sent his parents to play the wealth card, then make threats.

She dropped her hand and moved into the kitchen. She had groceries to put away. And dinner to make. Maybe she'd have a bowl of ice cream, enough to cool the fire still simmering inside.

After putting away the groceries, she skipped the ice cream and started dinner. In the next room, Addy read one of the children's books they'd brought from Mia's last night, her low voice a backdrop to the sounds of meal preparation. Shelby was half finished when a soft knock sounded on the door.

*Ryan.* She'd said he could come. That was before he'd gotten his parents involved. Now she had no problem with sending him back home.

As she stepped from the kitchen, Addy was watching her, eyes filled with questions.

"Ryan called me while I was at Safeway."

Addy furrowed her brow. "You're not letting him in, are you?"

"Absolutely not."

When she swung open the door, Ryan stood on the landing, holding a small plush teddy bear

and flashing her a smile warm enough to melt
the polar ice caps.

It didn't faze her. "Keep your gifts. As long
as I'm alive, no McConnell is going to raise
my niece."

The smile fell from his face. A second later,
she slammed the door with a boom that reverberated through the apartment.

Addy gave her a sharp nod. "Ryan's a good-
looking guy. He has a way with women. But you
can't trust him. The fact that he wants Chloe
makes him our enemy."

Shelby pursed her lips and headed for the
kitchen. Soon, the adrenaline that had pumped
through her system dissipated, leaving her more
zapped.

At least she didn't have to cook for Ryan.
Once dinner was over, she could chill. Maybe
put on a movie, something she could lose herself in.

No, she was an aunt now, and this was her
first opportunity to begin bonding with her
niece. How did one connect with a fifteen-
month-old? She had no clue. When Lauren
had left home and Shelby became responsible
for Mia's care, Mia had been six. Six-year-olds
played dolls, dress-up, games, make-believe.
Fifteen-month-olds did none of that.

Ryan would know what to do with her. He

had the job of uncle down pat. He also wanted to protect them. He'd proved that last night. Having him coming around on a regular basis would provide a wonderful sense of security.

But Addy was right. Ryan was their enemy. And she'd best remember that.

Chivalrous acts, good looks and warm smiles aside.

Ryan stared at the closed door, feeling as if he'd been beamed into the twilight zone. He'd just spoken with her a little over an hour ago. How could things have gone that far south so quickly?

He raised a fist to knock again, then lowered his hand. Whatever had happened, she wasn't going to be any more receptive now than she'd been a few seconds ago.

He headed back down the stairs, reviewing their phone conversation. He'd asked if he could visit Chloe, and aside from a soft sigh, Shelby hadn't voiced any objections.

Why would she tell him he could come, then turn him away after he'd driven all the way from the base in Bremerton? Not just turn him away, but slam the door in his face, as if he'd done something to offend her.

Mia had enjoyed creating drama. He'd never been on the receiving end of her outbursts, but he'd witnessed several temper tantrums involving other people. Maybe it was a family trait.

Based on their brief interactions, that wasn't how he would have pegged Shelby. Of course, he'd been wrong about people before. Especially women. Sometimes a pretty face could make a man's brain disengage. Though he liked to think otherwise, he probably wasn't any more immune than the next guy.

He cranked the Equinox and backed from the space. Now what?

He'd proceed the same as before and work on getting custody. Maybe not sole custody, but at least joint. His chances would be as good as hers.

Except his family was likely under investigation for Chloe's mother's murder. That would be a huge strike against him. His best option was still playing nice with Shelby. But how was he supposed to do that when she wouldn't even talk to him?

He headed down Bendigo toward the interstate. That had been a wasted trip. The last thing he'd expected was being turned away at the door. Her words still rang in his ears—*no McConnell is ever going to raise my niece.*

Since his brother was in jail, Ryan was the only McConnell in line for custody. Unless…

His jaw sagged. His father had paid Shelby

a visit. He was sure of it. Mia had mentioned bringing Chloe to visit his father and stepmother at their estate. Maybe there would be two other players in the custody battle.

Now Shelby's reaction made sense. Unless his old man had changed a lot in the past twenty years, he didn't play nice with anybody.

Ryan floored the accelerator, and the Equinox sped up the I-90 ramp. His only shot at talking to his father would be overtaking him before he reached the estate. Wrought iron wrapped the entire grounds, with an electronic gate guarding the long, curved drive. It was a gate that would never open for him. His father had made that clear when Ryan had announced his intentions to join the Navy instead of working in the family business.

Authorities had investigated the McConnell empire several times over the years, trying to find a connection to the Mafia. There wasn't any. Robert McConnell led a homegrown organized-crime outfit. And he was smart enough to always cover his tracks. That had been the case when Ryan lived at home and, based on what he'd read over the past twenty years, was still the case.

Ryan clicked on his signal and slid the SUV between two cars traveling in the far-left lane. At the tail end of rush hour, the crush of traffic was beginning to lessen, which would make catching up with his father easier.

He didn't even know what the man drove. Ryan hadn't seen him since he'd walked away twenty years ago. His father had pulled out every weapon in his arsenal to convince Ryan to stay. First, he'd used the promise of wealth and power. Then guilt. Then came the threats. Ryan had known enough about his father's business to be afraid. For months afterward, he'd looked over his shoulder, half convinced that someday the world would read about him in the news, the victim of an unsolved murder or apparent suicide.

Instead of acting on those threats, the old man had severed that father-son relationship. Even in the almost two-year time span since Ryan returned to the area, their paths hadn't crossed. Ryan made frequent trips into Seattle, but in a city with a population of more than seven hundred thousand, it was easy to avoid one another.

By the time he exited I-90, he hadn't approached any vehicles likely to contain his father. Visibility wasn't great. It was only six thirty, but the sun had set some time ago. Daylight saving time was still a few days away. Whatever the man was driving, it would be flashy and new. And expensive. He'd always appreciated nice things and enjoyed displaying them for others.

Several minutes later, Ryan made a left onto Lake Washington Boulevard. A vehicle traveled some distance ahead of him—something sleek and low to the ground, based on the taillight configuration.

He stepped on the gas and drew closer. It was a yellow Lamborghini Aventador. A ride fit for his father's tastes.

He held back through two more turns. When the vehicle's brake lights lit up again, Ryan tightened his hands on the wheel. His family's estate was just ahead. The signal clicked on, and Ryan backed off a little more. No sense alerting his father yet.

The sports car turned, and the wrought-iron gate a short distance off the road swung open slowly. Ryan didn't execute his own turn until the Lamborghini had almost cleared it. Then he stomped on the accelerator again, barely making it through before the gate closed.

The Lamborghini's brake lights came on, and it jerked to a halt. Seconds ticked past. His father didn't move. He'd probably already alerted security. And he was likely retrieving his own weapon. He didn't go anywhere unarmed.

Soon headlights moved toward them from the

direction of the house. The oncoming vehicle stopped, and one of his father's security people exited, weapon drawn.

Ryan stepped from the Equinox, hands raised to show he was unarmed. "I'm Ryan McConnell." The man wouldn't shoot without a directive. And if the senior McConnell wanted him dead, it would have happened a long time ago. "I'm here to talk to my father."

Ryan continued forward, his gait slow and even, his demeanor nonthreatening. The man stood stiff and alert, weapon aimed at Ryan's chest. A tense silence pressed down on them, holding back the faraway sounds of traffic and an even more distant lone siren. Above, the sky had deepened to dark charcoal, dotted with the occasional star. There was no moon.

Ryan stopped next to the Lamborghini, hands still raised. The headlights of the security vehicle washed through the windshield, bathing his father in their glow. He wasn't alone. Ryan's stepmother sat in the passenger seat.

His father reached for the handle, and Ryan stepped back as the driver's door opened. The older man swung out his legs, then unfolded to his full height. His hair had gone from dark to gray, with a smattering of brown, and time had forged a few more lines into his face. Judging from the coldness in his eyes, he still made a formidable foe.

The older man's jaw tightened. "Get off my property."

"We need to talk."

"You made your choice twenty years ago. I have nothing to say to you."

"Then listen."

His father crossed his arms. He'd either left his weapon in the car or had it hidden beneath his jacket. But his eyes held the same animosity they'd held two decades earlier. Back then, disappointment had tempered it. Now that disappointment was gone, and all that remained was hatred.

"You've got one minute." Ice laced his tone.

"Fine. I get it that Chloe's your granddaughter. I'll even accept that you've gotten attached to her. But Shelby is her aunt, and you're not going to take Chloe away from her." Because if Shelby lost the battle, he would, too.

"Boy, you're sticking your nose in where it doesn't belong."

"What happens to Chloe *is* my business. She's my niece." And he'd do anything in his power to make sure Robert McConnell didn't raise her. It was one thing he and Shelby agreed on.

His father's eyes narrowed. "You've said your piece. Now get off my property."

Ryan moved a step closer. "Stay away from Shelby, or I'll have her file a restraining order against you."

"Don't threaten me, boy."

"I'm not your boy."

The man's lips curled back in a sneer. "You're right. I only have one son."

"And he's locked up for the next decade or two. Enjoy that relationship."

The older man flinched, almost imperceptibly. Ryan had struck where it hurt—his father's only failures. Two sons, each a massive disappointment, for opposite reasons.

In elementary school, Ryan had looked up to the man with little-boy innocence. By the time he'd reached junior high, that innocence was gone. His father had begun to groom him, teaching him what it meant to be a McConnell. He'd taken Ryan to his clubs in Vegas, Reno, Portland and LA and walked him through in the morning hours, before the employees and any of the girls arrived. In the silence and stillness, a heavy air had hung over the empty establishments—dark and dangerous, but intriguing.

Ryan had also observed some meetings. The adults had talked in code, the phrases tough and mysterious, their meanings too obscure for his young brain to interpret. But one word always stood out. Every one of those intimidating men called his father "boss," a title that would one day be his.

The power was heady. But another influence pulled him in the opposite direction—Kyle's family. His father forbade the friendship, but his mother encouraged it. So weekends with his mom usually included time with the Gordons. In the end, Kyle's father won the battle for his future. The man was nothing that his own father was. And everything he was not.

Ryan spun and walked back to the Equinox, ultra-aware of the pistol locked on his back. When he climbed into his vehicle and shut the door, a tense breath escaped. The hedges on each side of the drive kept him from turning around easily, but after executing a seven-or nine-point turn, he headed back toward the gate. It swung open in front of him. Seconds later, he pulled onto the road and accelerated, the engine revving as he left his childhood home behind.

Chloe's custody should be an open-and-shut case. Shelby was the obvious choice. Or he was. Or both of them. But he couldn't say for sure that every judge in the district was beyond accepting bribes. If there was one that could be bought, his father would find a way to make sure he got the case.

But that wasn't all that weighed on him. He knew what his father was capable of. He just wasn't sure how far he was willing to go to get what he wanted this time.

Ryan was the man's flesh and blood. His father couldn't order the trigger pulled, or pull it himself, without some agonizing.

Shelby didn't have that advantage. Neither had the others who had crossed his father over the years. Men whose bodies had ended up in a back alley, or the Sammamish River, or locked in their own vehicles with a bullet through the head. Others had simply disappeared. There was never any evidence pointing to Robert McConnell. He was too good. Too careful.

But Ryan knew it. And law enforcement knew it.

Like those before her, Shelby was an unwanted obstacle. His father's other victims would have recognized their mistakes and known the danger they were in.

Shelby didn't. And seeing the fierce protectiveness in her eyes when she'd insisted she was taking Chloe, she wouldn't give up the fight even if she did.

That left Ryan with one option. He needed to warn her, to convince her he was on her side. To do that, he was going to have to get her to hear him out. She already didn't trust him, so it wouldn't be easy.

In fact, now that his father had paid her a visit, it was going to be nearly impossible.

# THREE

Shelby sat at her desk, a stack of cash in front of her. Music blared through the diner, a 1980s tune. The girls insisted they could get through cleanup faster with peppy music. Today it was Jeri's turn to pick what played, so she'd brought in a Def Leppard CD. Not Shelby's first choice, but as long as the work was getting done, she could listen to anything.

She tore a deposit slip from the pad and laid it next to the stack of cash. After transferring the currency and coin figures from the Post-It onto the correct lines, she stuffed everything into the zippered bag and locked it in the safe. Tomorrow morning, she'd slip out and make the bank run.

When she exited the office, Jeri was mopping the diner floor in time to "Bringin' On the Heartbreak." Tessa and Pam were apparently working in the kitchen.

Shelby stepped through the swinging metal

doors, and Tessa looked up from the cast-iron griddle she was curing. An easy smile climbed up her cheeks. That wasn't unusual. Whatever the task, Tessa radiated cheer.

Hiring her to fill the position of assistant manager three months ago had been one of the best decisions Shelby had made. With Tessa in charge, everything seemed to run as smoothly in Shelby's absence as when she was there. Though Shelby hadn't gone on a real vacation in years, several situations recently had taken her away from the diner for the day.

Two weeks ago, it was Aunt Bea's funeral. This week, it was meeting with a child-custody lawyer and planning yet another funeral. Saturday, she would leave Tessa in charge again while she said her final goodbye to Mia. In the coming months, there were going to be more obligations—checkups for Chloe, lawyer appointments, court hearings, interviews with Child Services.

Meanwhile, she'd dig up all the dirt she could find on the McConnells. Addy had already given her Randall's history. He'd been in and out of trouble and finally gotten caught dealing heroin. According to Addy, Robert was just as bad, was maybe even Mafia. Shelby hoped Addy had exaggerated that part because of her obvious dislike for both Ryan and his brother.

Shelby didn't know much about Ryan. Addy had only said he was a ladies' man and couldn't be trusted. But her gut told her he wasn't like his father and brother. Maybe it was the seriousness in his eyes. Or the fact that he'd spent the past twenty years serving his country. Or the way he carried himself, with pride and honor.

But he was a McConnell, and she didn't trust him any more than she trusted the others.

The jangling of the phone blended with the blare of guitars pouring from the CD player. Shelby hit Pause before slipping behind the counter to take the call. They were technically closed—they had been for more than a half hour—but she'd have to take care of the caller eventually. Why not now?

She lifted the receiver from the cradle on the back wall and put it to her ear. "Aunt Bea's Diner."

"Shelby?"

She'd spoken with Ryan a grand total of three times, but she recognized his smooth, rich voice instantly. She lowered the phone. Before she could place it back on the hook, pleading words reached her.

"Please, don't hang up." The desperation in his tone drew her up short.

She brought the receiver back to her ear. "All

right." She'd let him have his say. Then she'd hang up on him.

"I couldn't figure out what happened last night." He was talking fast, words tumbling out. "My dad paid you a visit, didn't he?"

She rolled her eyes. "And you knew nothing about it."

"No, I didn't. I knew Mia visited them regularly, but I had no idea they'd try to take custody of Chloe. We can't let that happen, Shelby. We don't want my dad raising our niece."

The conviction in his tone sent uneasiness spiking through her. "What do you suggest?"

"That we file for joint custody."

She pursed her lips. The whole thing could be a con. Maybe he was manipulating her, trying to make her feel they were on the same side so she'd let down her guard.

"How do I know you're not working with your parents?"

"You don't. You'll have to trust me."

*Yeah, right.* "And if I don't?"

"My father will win. Neither of us have the means to fight him alone. We need to work together."

She closed her eyes. If only Aunt Bea was still alive. She'd been Shelby's sounding board more than once. She'd possessed quiet strength and infinite wisdom, both of which she'd attributed to her relationship with God. Shelby had never found that kind of faith, but she'd always admired what she'd seen in Aunt Bea.

"I paid my father a visit last night." His words cut into her thoughts. "We hadn't spoken in twenty years."

*What?* And Ryan was critical of her for not staying in contact with Mia. "You live an hour apart."

"I'm the oldest child. My dad planned for me to work with him, to eventually take over his clubs. I wanted nothing to do with them. When I joined the Navy, he disowned me. The only way I got to speak with him last night was by following him onto his property before the electronic gate could close. His security person had a pistol aimed at me the whole time."

She lifted her eyebrows. She wasn't about to trust him, but what he was saying was too unbelievable to make up.

"My father is a dangerous man, Shelby." Urgency slipped into his voice. "Whether he's behind Mia's murder or not, the fact that you're fighting him for custody of Chloe puts your life in danger."

She closed her eyes and slouched against the counter. She'd always avoided trouble and minded her own business. How could this be happening?

She liked to think she was a good judge of

character. But people like the McConnells were way out of her league.

Ryan had said to trust him. For now, it looked like she had no choice. "What do we do?"

"We come up with an arrangement we can agree on, then present a united front."

Jeri wheeled the mop bucket to the far side of the floor to finish the last ten-foot strip. The lack of music didn't seem to be slowing her down. As soon as Shelby finished with Ryan, she'd take the player off Pause and check Pam's progress in the kitchen. In another fifteen minutes, they should all be out of there.

"How would the joint custody work?" she asked.

"Maybe you have her one week, I have her the next, with visitation in between."

"That might work." Shelby would do whatever was best for her niece. If that meant sharing her with Ryan, so be it. Once the little girl started kindergarten, he'd have to be content with weekends. Or move to the same school district.

Whatever they worked out, Addy would be Chloe's constant. She'd already said that where Chloe went, she went.

Last night, the three of them had watched a movie after all—Disney's *Frozen*. Addy had thrown several children's DVDs in with Chloe's other items. While the movie played, Addy had held Chloe, and Shelby had sat next to them. Several times, Chloe had let Shelby take her hand. Baby steps.

"Did you want to try that visit again?" If what he said was true, she almost felt bad for turning him away.

"If you didn't offer, I was going to ask." The relief in his tone was obvious. "I'll head over when I get off duty. It'll be around the same time as last night." He paused. "Thank you, Shelby."

Warmth swelled inside. She didn't have Aunt Bea's connection to the Almighty, but her gut said she'd made the right decision.

As she finished the call, Tessa walked out of the kitchen and began positioning chairs where the floor had dried. Shelby hung up the phone and released the pause button. "Bringin' On the Heartbreak" resumed, the blast of sound jarring after the relative silence.

When she poked her head into the kitchen, everything looked good. The dishwashers were on their dry cycles and Pam was spraying disinfectant on the work surfaces. Shelby helped her staff finish the chores, then ejected the CD. Muffled screams came from upstairs.

Tessa gave Shelby a sympathetic smile. "Your niece isn't a happy camper."

"Addy will get her settled down." She always did. It wasn't that Shelby didn't want to soothe the little girl's troubles, Chloe just wouldn't let her. Someday.

She handed the CD to Jeri and followed the women to the door. After locking it behind them, she clicked off the lights. As she ascended the stairs, the wails grew louder.

An hour ago, Chloe had been fine. Addy had popped down to show her off to the staff and the last straggling customers. When Addy had asked, Shelby had told her they were working on closing and she'd be up in an hour. Either the nap Addy had planned for Chloe hadn't happened, or Chloe had awoken too early.

At the top of the stairs, Shelby opened the door and stepped into the hall. The screams came from the living room. When she rounded the corner, her knees went weak. The coffee table was flipped on its side. Aunt Bea's Tiffany lamp was lying in front of the end table, colorful pieces of glass scattered across the hardwood floor.

Shelby rushed into the room, her heart pounding. Addy sat on the floor, holding a screaming Chloe. Next to them was a ring of keys with a pink tube that looked a lot like a pepper spray canister. Twenty feet away, the exterior door was wide open.

Shelby dropped to her knees in front of Addy. "What happened?"

"He tried to take Chloe."

"Who?"

"I don't know." Hysteria raised her voice an octave. "He wanted to know where Mia's phone was. He hit me."

Shelby rose and ran onto the landing. The alley below was empty. The assailant had likely crossed the railroad tracks and disappeared into the woods.

After locking the door, she returned to where Addy sat and took her screaming niece. "Have you called the police?"

"No."

"Do it now." They could sort out what happened once law enforcement arrived.

Addy rose and walked into the kitchen while Shelby paced the floor with Chloe. The little girl wasn't any more distraught than she'd been when Addy had held her, but she wasn't calming down, either.

Shelby rubbed Chloe's back, making slow circles. "Shh, sweetie. It's okay. Aunt Shelby's got you."

When pacing didn't work, she sank onto the love seat. As she rocked back and forth, the little girl's wails quieted to sobs, each ragged breath shaking her body. Chloe slipped her thumb into her mouth and pressed the side of her face against Shelby's chest. Shelby held her more tightly, a sense of protectiveness surging through her. Her niece had been with her less than forty-eight hours, and she'd already planted herself deep in Shelby's heart.

Addy returned and sat on the couch, dropping her phone next to her. "The police are on the way."

Shelby nodded. "What happened? How did this person get in?"

"He knocked on the door. I thought it was you."

"When I'm coming from the diner, I use the inside stairs." But Addy wouldn't know that. Yesterday Shelby had gone shopping after closing and used the other door.

"Who was it?"

"I don't know." She pressed shaking fingers to her face. Her right cheek was red and starting to swell. "He was wearing a ski mask."

"What did he say?"

"He demanded—"

Addy's phone buzzed with an incoming text. She frowned and picked it up. For the next several seconds, her thumbs slid over the screen. Then she laid it facedown on the couch.

"Who was that?" Maybe it was none of her

business. But she wasn't leaving any questions unanswered.

"A friend. We were talking about doing something tonight, but I told him this is a bad time."

Sirens sounded in the distance, increasing in volume. Shelby continued to rub Chloe's back. Except for an occasional hiccup, she was silent and still.

"What did the guy with the mask say?"

"He wanted Mia's phone."

"Why?"

"I don't know. Maybe there was something on it. I told him I didn't have it. Then he hit me."

"Where was Chloe?" Based on how upset she'd been, she'd probably witnessed the entire thing.

"On the couch. I had trouble getting her to go down for her nap, so I was reading to her. When I couldn't give him the phone, he tried to take Chloe."

The sirens grew louder, one apparently coming from the back. When they died, Addy moved to the door. The responding officer would get the rest of the details. Meanwhile, if Chloe was ready for a nap, Shelby would put her in bed, then round up something to eat.

Addy opened the door and called a greeting. The thudding of heavy footfalls on the steps followed. When Shelby rose, Chloe's thumb remained in her mouth, her other arm hanging limp at her side. Shelby walked into the bedroom that Chloe and Addy shared.

It wasn't the ideal setup. Chloe needed her own space. But the apartment only had two bedrooms. When Addy had insisted on setting up the Pack 'N Play in the guest bedroom, Shelby hadn't argued. If Chloe awoke in the middle of the night frightened, she'd feel more secure knowing Addy was with her.

Shelby stopped next to the portable playpen and bent over the side rail to lay Chloe in the bottom. Her eyes opened for a moment before falling closed again, and her mouth moved in a sucking motion. After picking up the stuffed seal from the bottom of the playpen, Shelby slid it under Chloe's arm, then positioned the lightweight baby blanket over her.

For several moments, she stood watching her niece sleep. Brownish-red curls fell across Chloe's face. Her eyes were closed and her mouth relaxed around the thumb. She was so young and innocent.

And Shelby was responsible for her well-being—mental, physical and emotional. Never in her life had she felt so inadequate.

She drew in a stabilizing breath and moved toward the door. A framed picture sat atop the chest of drawers. She'd asked the detectives if she could take it. Since it had been in Chloe's room, which was untouched, they'd given her permission. It was a picture of Mia holding Chloe. Had Mia felt inadequate, too?

Shelby touched a finger to the glass. As always, Mia was beautiful. She couldn't take a bad picture if she tried. But upon a closer look, her makeup was a little too heavy, her smile a little too fake and her eyes a little too empty.

Shaking off a sudden sense of melancholy, Shelby stepped into the hall. When she returned to the living room, Addy was sitting on the love seat, relaying what had happened. Dave Jenkins was on the sofa adjacent to her in his crisp dark uniform. In his midfifties and single, he was one of the officers who frequented Aunt Bea's.

He stopped writing and ran his fingers through his thinning hair, making some of the shorter strands on top stand up. Shelby gave him a nod and headed toward the kitchen. As she passed the door, a soft knock sounded. Ryan was almost twenty minutes earlier than he'd estimated.

When she opened the door, it wasn't Ryan who stood there. The man was younger, closer to her age, with blond hair on the long side and a day's worth of stubble. Ryan had him beat by only an inch or two, but probably outweighed him by fifty pounds.

She lifted an eyebrow. "Can I help you?"

"Is Addy here?"

Shelby cast a glance at Addy. She didn't look happy. Her eyes were narrowed, her mouth tight. "I told you not to come."

The stranger stepped inside. "I was worried. I had to make sure you're okay."

"I'm fine."

Her curt tone didn't deter him. Neither did Dave, with his badge. "Your face is red. You're hurt."

Addy had referred to him as a friend, but that wasn't how he was looking at her.

"I told you I'm fine." Her tone held a solid dose of annoyance. Unlike Mia, Addy apparently didn't like to be fussed over. Unfortunately, her friend seemed the type to do just that. Creases of worry framed his frown.

Addy turned her attention back to Dave, ignoring her unwanted visitor. "I don't know what's on Mia's cell phone. This incident is probably related to her murder. I'm guessing there are incriminating pictures. If they're erased from her phone, you should look for a Google account or somewhere else she might have stored photos on the cloud."

As she talked, her friend made no attempt to leave. Shelby wasn't going to throw him out. Once Dave left, Addy could do as she pleased.

The guy seemed harmless. He stood silently against the wall, watching Addy with puppy-dog eyes. As if there was no one else in the room.

A pang of jealousy shot through Shelby, unwanted and irrational. She turned and walked into the kitchen. She didn't want anyone to look at her that way. At least not now. Her life was in too much turmoil. The few guys she'd dated had expected to be the center of her universe. She hadn't had the time or patience for that level of possessiveness then, and she certainly didn't now.

She pulled the pack of ground beef from the fridge and laid an onion on the counter. Busy was okay. It was that sense of not being in control that was unsettling. The moment she'd learned of Mia's murder, her world had slanted sideways. It still hadn't righted itself.

She placed a skillet on the stove, then tore into the cellophane covering the beef. Eventually, she'd settle into a routine. Instead of her and Aunt Bea, her family unit would consist of her and Chloe. And Addy. Ryan would probably join them on holidays.

She didn't know about her mom and dad. They'd left Seattle for Arizona two years ago, tired of the city, the winters and the rain. They hadn't made it back for a visit yet. Shelby had hoped the sunshine would lift her mom's spirits. Based on Shelby's monthly phone calls, it hadn't.

While the beef simmered, she diced the onion, relieved that Ryan was on his way. She'd always felt safe in North Bend. But Ryan's warnings about his father had scared her more than she wanted to admit. And the attack on Addy had sent her uneasiness skyrocketing.

Was the senior McConnell responsible? He was determined to get Chloe. He'd made that clear yesterday. But why would he resort to kidnapping when they hadn't even begun the legal process?

Maybe there was more to it than that. If Robert McConnell *was* the one who'd had Mia killed, maybe he sent one of his thugs to get her phone, and when Addy didn't produce it, the guy tried to come up with a bargaining chip—the kid for the phone. Maybe the two events weren't even connected. What if Mia had more than one enemy?

She heaved a sigh. The unanswered questions were making her brain hurt.

Once Ryan got there, she'd discuss everything with him. She didn't have to do this alone. Some of the heaviness lifted at the thought.

Unfortunately, she didn't even know if she could trust him.

* * *

Ryan exited I-90 onto 202 and headed into North Bend. Mount Si stood in the distance, blanketed by clouds. Behind and to the left, the sun sat low on the horizon. Soon he'd be holding his niece. Provided nothing had happened since he'd talked with Shelby.

The conversation had turned out better than he'd hoped. Keeping her from hanging up on him had been a huge accomplishment. She was still guarded. It had come through in her tone. But she was willing to work with him. He just had to make sure nothing shattered the tentative trust they were building. Not just for Chloe's sake, but for Shelby's own safety.

Ryan traveled slowly down North Bend Way. The diner was ahead on the left, with parallel parking spots in front. The block was like several others downtown—establishments pressed together in a row-house style. Aunt Bea's Diner was on the end.

He chose a spot in the largely empty lot at the side of the building. The last remnants of daylight were fading fast and the parking lot's lights were already on.

Ryan stepped around the corner. An alley stretched along the rear of the building, interrupted in the distance by a side street before continuing through the next block. Angled parking spaces lined the outer edge of the alley.

Shelby's Town Car was there, next to Addy's Camaro. Two other vehicles weren't familiar—a gray Challenger and, beyond that, a dark SUV. As he drew closer, dread circled through him. On the side of the SUV, white-and-gold letters spelled Snoqualmie Police North Bend. The last time he'd shown up where there were cops, someone was dead.

He hit the stairs at a run, then rapped on the door. Finally, it swung inward, and Shelby stood wiping her hands on a dish towel. An aroma wafted from the apartment, a scent that should have been pleasant. Instead, it sent a wave of nausea through him.

Shelby stepped back. "Come in. We had an incident."

Ryan moved inside, his heart pounding. The room was obviously the scene of a struggle, with the coffee table tipped over and a lamp shattered. Addy sat on the love seat, a uniformed officer adjacent to her. Addy's friend stood with his back against the wall. Ryan had met him several times at Mia's place. Barry, if he remembered right.

"Where is Chloe?"

Shelby tilted her head toward the hall. "Taking a nap."

Ryan released a tension-filled breath. Chloe was safe.

"What happened?"

Shelby motioned for him to follow her. In the kitchen, steam rose from a skillet holding simmering hamburger and onions. A large covered pot sat on a hot burner, a box of lasagna pasta nearby.

"I'll let Addy fill you in over dinner, but I'll give you the abridged version."

He nodded. She was inviting him to stay. Good. He'd need all the time he could get to convince her to accept his protection. Apparently, she wasn't any safer in North Bend than Mia had been in Seattle. He'd put his Glock in the Equinox's glove box. From now on, it would be at his side. If Shelby would let him, he was going to start sleeping on her couch.

After draining the hamburger and adding tomato paste and spices, she dropped the pasta into the now boiling water. "I was downstairs, getting everything cleaned up and prepped for tomorrow. Someone knocked on the door up here. When Addy opened it, a guy in a ski mask barged in."

Ryan clenched his fists. "She opened the door for a stranger?" The woman had no sense.

"She thought it was me."

He drew in a calming breath. Escaping to a

small, quaint town had probably lured Addy into a false sense of security. Hopefully she'd learned her lesson. Until they found out who'd murdered Mia and why, nowhere was safe.

Shelby removed salad ingredients from the fridge and laid a cutting board on the counter. She'd just gotten started when the police officer appeared in the doorway. He gave Ryan a nod, then turned his attention to Shelby.

"I'm finished with Ms. Sorenson's statement. What can you tell me?"

Shelby put down the knife. "Not much. I was downstairs cleaning the diner. When I came up, Chloe was screaming, and Addy was on the floor holding her. I ran to the open door, but whoever had come in was gone."

"You didn't hear anything when you were downstairs?"

"No. We always do cleanup to music." She gave the officer a sheepish smile. "Loud music. As soon as I turned it off, I heard Chloe screaming, but I thought she was just unhappy. When I got upstairs, I found everything the way it was when you arrived. I took Chloe and got her calmed down. She fell asleep in my arms, and I laid her in her crib."

Her gaze shifted in Ryan's direction and he smiled. Those last details were as much for him as for the cop. Apparently, Chloe was starting to warm up to her. It had happened faster than he'd expected. He wasn't sure how he felt about it.

The officer finished jotting notes in his pad, then closed it. "Ms. Sorenson said he was wearing gloves, so I won't dirty your place trying to lift prints."

"Okay." She led him to the door and bid him farewell, with a promise to call if they had anything else to report.

Ryan reached for the knob. "I'll be right back." Someone had barged in and attacked Addy. He wasn't going to wait until tomorrow to start carrying his weapon.

Barry pushed himself away from the wall. "I'm stepping out for a few minutes, too."

Ryan descended the steps, the younger man's lighter tread right behind him. When he reached his vehicle, Barry stopped beside him.

"Can I talk to you?"

Ryan turned to face him. "Sure."

Barry shifted his weight from one foot to the other. "I don't know if you realize it, but I... I'm in love with Addy. I think she feels the same about me."

Ryan nodded. How Barry felt about Addy was obvious to anyone with eyes and half a brain.

Barry's gaze slid to the trees, which now looked like a dark wall, their tops blurring into an equally dark sky. "I'm still in shock that I've actually landed a woman like her."

Ryan waited for him to continue. Where was Barry headed with this? Several more seconds passed in silence. "Is there something you want to tell me?"

Barry met his eyes, then looked down at his feet. "I can't compete with you. I'm an engineering major. A math-and-science geek. You're like the jock, the captain of the football team." Barry lifted his gaze, his eyes holding a silent plea. "If you show women any attention, they flock to you."

Ryan's jaw dropped. His first instinct was to laugh, but the worry on the other man's face stopped him before the first snicker could escape. "Trust me, you have nothing to worry about. I'm no more interested in Addy than she is in me."

Barry's eyebrows lifted as a cautious hope seemed to temper the worry. "You're sure?"

"I'm positive. You're not in competition with me."

Barry nodded slowly. "Please don't change your mind. Addy is everything to me."

Ryan rested a hand on the other man's shoulder. "I understand. Just concern yourself with making her happy."

Barry headed back toward the steps, and

Ryan retrieved his weapon, clipping the holster to his belt. Once he dropped his jacket back into place, it was hidden from view. When he entered the apartment, Addy was leading Barry toward the door, his mouth set in a frown.

"Can I just hang with you? I feel bad."

Addy shot him a warning glare. "I told you not to come." She glanced at Shelby, then softened her tone. "Look, Barry, I appreciate your concern, but other than being tired, I'm fine. I just want to chill."

Barry followed Addy onto the landing, where she closed the door behind him. Several minutes passed before she came back in. Maybe she'd been trying to let him down easy. Ryan felt sorry for him.

Shelby frowned at Addy through the kitchen doorway. "That poor guy has it bad."

Addy shrugged and tossed her hair behind her shoulders. Having a love-struck admirer obviously didn't bother her. She was used to it.

It wasn't just her looks; it was everything about her. She acted like flirting was a competitive sport and she was going for first place. She'd tried it on him, too, when they'd first met. The cold shoulder he'd given her had relayed a clear "Thanks, but no thanks." An undercurrent of tension had flowed between them ever since. Men didn't turn down advances from a woman like Addy.

Fifteen years ago, he might have fallen for it. Not now. He was more immune than the average guy to the wiles of beautiful women. Someday he might let down his guard and risk his heart. Maybe even marry again. But it would be someone his own age, settled and mature. Faithful.

Addy poked her head into the kitchen. "What's left to do?"

"Finish the salad, assemble the lasagna and set the table."

Ryan backed up to allow Addy access to the kitchen, then leaned against the doorjamb. "How long will you let Chloe sleep?"

Shelby cast him a glance over one shoulder. "I'll have to get her up to eat. But the glass needs to be cleaned up first."

"We'll let her sleep another thirty minutes," Addy said. "Any longer and we'll never get her to bed tonight."

Ryan nodded. The voice of experience. Shelby probably hadn't considered it. Not that he would have, either. His frequent visits hadn't prepared him for full-time parenting any more than Shelby's absence had prepared her. With Addy around, neither of them had to worry about it.

He pushed himself away from the doorjamb. "I'll clean up the glass."

Shelby retrieved a broom and dustpan from a closet and handed them to him. After righting the coffee table and disposing of the remnants of the lamp, he stepped into the hall. Three in the kitchen was too crowded. The space wasn't that large.

Actually, the whole apartment wasn't very big. But it was clean and comfortable. Cozy. The decor was a hodgepodge of colors and styles, old and new, knickknacks likely chosen and displayed for their sentimental value rather than to complement a decorating scheme.

Ryan stopped at a door that was open about three inches and slowly pushed it wide. On the opposite wall, a double window faced North Bend Way, but the shades were drawn, casting the room in shadow. A full-size bed sat against one wall, the playpen adjacent. Chloe was lying in the middle, her hair a mass of copper-colored curls, her body an elongated lump beneath a pink-and-white blanket.

He moved closer until he stood right beside her. Love swelled in his chest. "My dad's not going to get you."

For several minutes, he watched her sleep, the blanket rising and falling with her breaths. He had no clue how to raise a child. He'd never even helped with his younger brother and sister. His family had had nannies for those chores. If Shelby was as inexperienced as he was, they'd be figuring things out together.

He turned from his sleeping niece and moved into the hall. When he reached the living room, soft humming drifted to him from the kitchen. There was something appealing about the sound. It transformed the ambience of the place, filling it with a cozy warmth that made him want to stay.

When he entered the kitchen, Addy had apparently finished the salad and tucked it away in the fridge. Shelby was sliding a lasagna-filled baking dish into the oven. She glanced up at him, and the humming stopped.

"So what happened today?" He was ready for the unabridged version.

Addy walked past him into the living room. "A guy in a hoodie and ski mask came to the door and demanded I give him Mia's cell phone." She sank onto the love seat. "But the police took it the night she died."

Shelby followed and sat on the couch. "Mia insisted there was something shady going on at the club. It sounds like she got pictures. Or someone thinks she did."

Ryan sat next to her. When she'd first told the police what Mia had said, he'd thought it was a ploy to take his niece. Not anymore. "Any idea who it was?"

"All I could see was his eyes." Addy rose and started to pace. "I was too scared to even notice their color. His voice was normal, not high or low. No accent."

"Any chance it was Ryan's dad?" Shelby's eyes shifted to his.

He'd had the same thought.

"The guy was shorter than Mr. McConnell, stockier." Addy stopped at one of the two front windows and peered out. "When I wouldn't give him Mia's phone, he hit me." She dropped the curtain back into place and turned toward them, one hand against her cheek. Her makeup didn't hide the redness.

She resumed her pacing. "Then he headed straight for Chloe."

Ryan almost choked. "What?" Shelby's earlier version had omitted that detail.

"She was on the couch, where I'd been reading to her. I jumped on the guy's back, screaming, and he spun and threw me off. On the way down, I caught the edge of the coffee table and flipped it. My keys were sitting there." She pointed to the end table positioned between the couch and love seat. "I have pepper spray on my key ring, so I grabbed it and lunged for him. I got him right in the eyes."

Ryan's chest clenched. "You didn't spray Chloe, did you?"

"No. When I lunged, that put me between him and Chloe. Chloe's fine."

The reality of what had almost happened hit him hard. If Addy had put her keys in her purse or left them in the bedroom or anywhere else, Chloe would be gone.

Addy continued, still pacing. "He grabbed his eyes, spun around and lost his balance. That's how the lamp got broken. I sprayed him again, and he stumbled to the door and left."

She stopped at the same window to peer outside. "I'm so scared. What if he comes back and tries again?" When she turned back around, her eyes were wide, the terror of those moments reflected in their depths.

Ryan sprang to his feet. "We have to take Chloe away. Whoever is after her knows she's here."

Shelby stood, too, and flung her arms wide. "I can't leave. I have a business to run."

"Then let me take her."

She frowned up at him. "Do you live on base?"

"I rent a condo about two miles from it." With the exception of his first two years, he'd chosen to collect the housing allowance and live off base.

"Then Chloe won't be any safer with you than she is with me."

"How do you figure that?"

"You work. Unless you're planning to go AWOL."

"I have three weeks of leave built up. I've already put in for it."

"And in the meantime? If you lived on base, it would be different. No one would be able to drive in without going through security."

She was right. He couldn't protect her while he was on duty. Maybe he could talk to some of his Navy buddies whose shifts didn't overlap with his. Several had kids. But those guys spent their spare time with their own families. The ones who didn't wouldn't want to be tied down with a little one.

Shelby moved to stand in front of him. In this light, her eyes looked darker, the gold flecks turning to brown and blending with the green around them. "When I'm working, I'm right downstairs. Addy won't open the door for anyone. And no more loud music during cleanup."

"Do you have a security system?"

"I'll get one installed."

"Monitored."

"Agreed."

Addy stepped forward and rested a hand on Shelby's shoulder. "Let me take her. My parents have a farm in Idaho. She'll be safe there." The urgency in her tone was reflected on her face.

Ryan's stomach twisted at the thought of anyone taking his niece several hundred miles away. What if someone followed? Regardless of what she'd done with the pepper spray today, Addy wasn't qualified to provide the protection Chloe needed.

"Shelby will get the security system installed, and I'll see how quickly they'll approve my leave time." Maybe he'd look into having someone watch her place, too. It wouldn't be cheap.

Were his father and stepmother desperate enough to try to kidnap Chloe? That didn't make sense. They'd have to keep her hidden. They'd eventually get caught and go to jail. Then they'd lose her, anyway. His father hadn't avoided incarceration all these years by making stupid decisions.

But who else would want to take his little niece? It couldn't be for money. Neither he nor Shelby had the means to pay a ransom demand. Unless whoever was behind today's attack was close enough to know his father would likely cough up any amount of money to secure Chloe's safety.

Addy paced back to the window. "I don't like it at all." She swept aside the curtains. "If we stay here, we're nothing but sitting—"

Addy's sudden pause set off alarms in Ryan's mind. "What is it?"

"Someone's out there, across the street, under the tree." She gasped, spun away from the window and pressed her back against the wall. "He pointed a gun at me."

Ryan was beside her in three quick strides. Outside, a figure moved away, walking fast down the wide sidewalk on the opposite side of the road. He wore a trench coat, or maybe a raincoat. No ski mask. But the streetlights didn't provide enough illumination to identify him.

Ryan ran toward the door. "Call the police."

When he reached the bottom of the stairs, he charged down the alley, which was parallel to the road. At the end of the block, he zigzagged onto North Bend Way. The town's streets were laid out on a diagonal grid. The suspect was some distance ahead of him, running southeast, the long coat flowing behind him.

As Ryan pounded down the sidewalk, he popped his phone from its clip without breaking his stride. When the dispatcher came on, he relayed what he knew. As he finished, the man disappeared around a building.

"He just turned left on Bendigo." Ryan didn't know many of North Bend's street names, but this one he did. Also known as 202, it was the same road he'd taken from the interstate. When he rounded the corner, the assailant was only a half block ahead of him. Without looking back, the man ran down a smaller side street.

"He just took a left." Ryan sprinted closer, his breaths coming fast and hard. He squinted at the small green-and-white sign. "He's running northwest on Second Street."

As he approached the intersection, he cut through the Opus Bank property to shave off some distance. Sirens sounded nearby. He wouldn't engage. He'd just relay the suspect's whereabouts until the police arrived to apprehend him.

When the man disappeared down a side road, Ryan crossed the street and reached the intersection less than a half minute later. Sydney Avenue was devoid of life. This part of town was residential, with homes lining both sides of the road. About forty yards ahead, vehicles were parked bumper-to-bumper against the curb, forming a barrier along the sidewalk's edge almost to the end of the block.

A flash of movement some distance away drew his gaze. Just that quickly, the figure was gone. "I'm on Sydney now. The suspect might have turned right a block ahead." He couldn't say for sure. The shadows were too deep.

He moved forward at a jog, then slowed as he reached the rear quarter panel of the nearest vehicle. A stretch of fence bordered the sidewalk to his right, with bushes at the end. He moved past the next car, then drew to a stop, feeling hemmed in. It would be too easy for someone crouched between the vehicles to jump out and attack.

Movement to his right sent panic shooting through him. A figure sprang from behind a large bush. An arm shot out, swinging toward his face, but the movement was too quick for him to identify the object in the hand. He pivoted in time to keep his nose and facial bones intact.

The blow to the side of his head sent stars exploding across his vision and brought him to his knees. Darkness moved in from all sides. At some point, he'd dropped his phone, because it was no longer in his hand.

The dispatcher's voice sounded far away. "Are you there?"

He was in a crawling position, but his body ignored the commands his brain issued. "Help. I'm down."

He fell sideways, face against the rough pavement. Where was his assailant? Standing over him, pistol aimed?

Twenty years in the Navy and a twelve-month deployment to a war zone, and he was going to die on the streets of a quaint town like North Bend?

The pounding of retreating footsteps brought a mix of disappointment and relief. He'd lost the suspect and sent the police in the wrong direction.

He'd failed.

But he wasn't going to die tonight.

# FOUR

Shelby stood at an alarm keypad the following Monday afternoon, her thumb and index finger stroking her chin. The diner was closed, the tables behind her empty. The technician was nearby, his back to her. Lance, according to his introduction and the stitching on his shirt. He'd just instructed her how to program her code into the system.

Now she needed to come up with one, something easy to remember but difficult to guess. She'd avoid the combinations experts warned about—1234 or 2468 or a series of duplicate numbers. Her birth date was out, too. She had no idea what information whoever was threatening her could access.

She finally settled on 0621, Lauren's birth date. Since she and her older sister hadn't spoken in fifteen years, no one would try that one.

She punched in the numbers, following the

instructions Lance had given her. "Okay, I'm done." Now to program the apartment.

When Ryan had dashed out the door after the gunman Thursday night, the minutes had stretched into almost a half hour before she'd heard anything. He'd been struck and was sitting on the sidewalk dazed, refusing medical treatment and determined to return to her apartment. His assailant had gotten away. But the incident confirmed one thing—the shot that was fired last week hadn't been random. It had been intended for her.

After Thursday night's scare, calling an alarm company had been the first thing on her to-do list for the next morning. She'd gotten a hold of Sonitrol Pacific out of nearby Bellevue as soon as they'd opened. Fortunately, they'd had a cancellation for Monday and were able to work her into the schedule quickly.

She led Lance toward the kitchen and up the stairs to the apartment. He'd installed two separate systems, allowing the apartment to be armed when the diner was open. The system also had three cameras they could monitor through a phone or iPad.

When Shelby stepped into the living room, Ryan was sitting on the floor with Chloe, helping her build a Lincoln Log house. He'd started sleeping there Friday night, stretching his large form out on her couch.

Addy wasn't happy about it. Even now, she stood in the kitchen doorway, arms crossed and full lips formed in a pout. Someday Shelby would ask Ryan what had happened between them.

Or not. It was none of her business. They'd probably been an item then went through a nasty breakup. Obviously, Addy was still holding a grudge.

Despite Addy's unhappiness, Shelby was relieved to have Ryan there. It couldn't be easy for him. Even with the pillow and sheet she'd given him, he'd hardly looked comfortable. Thinking about the hour-and-a-half drive from the base made her appreciate his sacrifice even more.

Lance walked her through how to change a previously set code and program different ones for multiple users. As Addy returned to the kitchen to finish the meal she and Shelby had worked on together, Shelby stepped up to the pad. After a few seconds of pondering, she entered her father's birthday. Another unlikely combination. Her relationship with her dad wasn't much better than her relationship with her sister. But she at least talked to him on a semiregular basis.

When she walked back through the living

room, the mini construction project was almost finished. Chloe picked up a piece and handed it to Ryan, chattering in that sweet, little-girl voice.

"I know." Ryan placed it with the others. "This is the best house ever."

Chloe clapped her hands, and Shelby smiled, warmth spreading through her. Either he understood the unintelligible words or was great at pretending he did. He was so good with his little niece.

But it was more than that. He was a good-looking guy, and Shelby couldn't deny her attraction to him. There was something about a military man—the way he carried himself, the discipline and physical fitness, the attitude of service. The combination was irresistible.

If he'd joined the military right out of high school, that would put him at thirty-seven or thirty-eight. Ten or eleven years her senior.

She'd always been attracted to guys older than her. As a teenager, the ones her own age had seemed so immature, their lives revolving around music, fast cars and video games. She'd wondered if they'd ever grow up.

She hadn't had time for them, anyway. Between keeping up with her studies and being cook, maid, caretaker and nanny all rolled into one, the need for sleep crowded out the usual teenage interests.

She led Lance down the stairs to the diner, shaking off thoughts of Ryan. She'd dated a handful of guys over the years, but none of the relationships had gotten serious. That was fine with her. Aunt Bea's single life had always appealed to her more than her mother's. With a fifteen-year age difference, her dad had used his greater maturity to exercise his oppressive form of control over her mother from the moment they said "I do." Shelby was determined to avoid that trap. She hadn't sworn off men permanently, but she was good at listening to her brain instead of her heart.

Lance approached one of the diner tables where a clipboard sat, paperwork attached. "I think that does it. Call if you have any issues or questions." He handed her a business card.

After he'd processed her credit card payment and she'd signed the forms, he headed toward the door. Another unexpected expense.

Saturday, she'd gotten the funeral over with. It had been the longest half hour of her life. Now all she had left of her sister was a huge bill and the weight of grief and regret.

Mia hadn't had life insurance. Although Shelby had gotten her own small policy at age eighteen, she didn't blame Mia. Normal young people didn't prepare for the possibility of death. Now, between the funeral, the lawyer and the alarm system, her meager savings account was taking a hit. No, not a hit—a fatal blow.

She unlocked the diner's front door and watched Lance walk to his van. A Chevy Blazer was parked in the space in front of him. A man rounded the vehicle and approached, his demeanor all business. He was dressed in jeans and a polo shirt, with a clipboard in one hand.

"Shelby Adair?"

"Yes?"

"I'm a process server and have some documents for you."

He handed her several pages, then turned the clipboard toward her. "I need you to sign here that you received them."

She scrawled her name on the stamped line. After he noted the date and time, he bid her farewell. Once inside the diner, she scanned the top page. Her chest tightened.

What she held wasn't a shock. Mr. McConnell had warned her they would fight for custody. But holding the nonparent custody petition in her hand drew her insides into a knot. First thing tomorrow, she'd put all this into the hands of her lawyer.

Before heading for the stairs, she set the alarm. She'd be down before any of her staff arrived in the morning. She always was. And she was usually the last to leave in the afternoon. But she'd still have Tessa create a code of her own.

As far as the apartment, she'd make sure Addy had the ability to disarm the system. Since Addy would always be there when Ryan came and went, he wouldn't need a code.

She'd known him for only six days. That was how long she'd known Addy, too. But Ryan's family was likely responsible for her sister's death and his parents were trying to get custody of Chloe. Her gut told her she could trust him, but why jump the gun?

When she stepped into the apartment, the clinking of plates and silverware came from the kitchen. Addy was apparently setting the table. Ryan and Chloe had finished their project, and Chloe was disassembling it.

Ryan looked up at her with a smile that immediately faded. "What's wrong?"

For a guy, he was perceptive. "The battle with your parents has begun."

"What do you mean?" He pushed himself to his feet, lips pressed into a thin line.

She handed him the papers. "Looks like they got their case filed the same time as mine."

"If there are two different cases started, maybe they'll combine them."

"Maybe." She didn't know how that worked. All she knew was that less than a week had passed since Mia's murder, and she was already locked in a nasty legal battle.

She tipped her head toward the papers. "There's a subpoena for a DNA test, too."

"Already?"

"Yeah." Whether it was standard procedure to prepare everything at the same time, or the McConnells were trying to expedite things, she didn't know. Patience probably wasn't one of Robert McConnell's virtues.

She frowned. "I want to get it over with." She'd never been one to procrastinate. Besides, wrapping up the case while Robert McConnell was still under investigation for Mia's murder would increase her chances for victory.

Ryan's eyes met hers. "I'm going with you."

"Won't you be on duty?"

"I'll take off."

She drew her brows together. "Can you do that?"

"Yeah." He grinned. "It's the military, not prison."

"Speaking of prison, how are they going to get Randall's DNA? Addy said he's in jail."

Ryan frowned. His brother had probably been an embarrassment to him more than once.

"They have ways. My guess is they'll send someone to the jail to collect what they need."

Addy poked her head through the kitchen doorway. "There's no need for Ryan to take time off. I'll go with you."

"I'm going." The sternness in his tone discouraged any argument.

Addy spun and stalked back into the kitchen. The oven door creaked open and the dish of baked chicken came down on the stove harder than necessary.

Shelby winced, then raised her voice to carry to the other woman. "Ryan will be armed. It'll be safer for both you and Chloe. If you'd like to invite Barry over while you don't have the responsibility for Chloe, that's fine with me."

The kitchen was silent except for the clinking of utensils against stainless steel as Addy transferred food into serving bowls and the metallic thud of the empty pans slamming back down on the coiled burners. With Addy's animosity toward Ryan, choosing him over her on anything to do with Chloe was a surefire way to see Addy's moody side.

Ryan had been there for three nights, and already the tension was getting to her. She'd always been a peacemaker. When her father had railed at Lauren, Shelby had jumped in and tried to defend her.

When Lauren had left home at eighteen, Shelby had become the new target. Maybe Mia got it once Shelby became an adult. Since that was when Aunt Bea took ill and Shelby stepped in as caretaker, homemaker and diner manager, she wouldn't know.

But it wasn't likely. Mia had always managed to escape the worst of their father's criticism and unrealistic expectations, landing the role of pampered princess. Some things in life weren't fair.

Ryan picked up Chloe. "Come on, sweetie. Let's wash your hands for supper."

He disappeared down the hall, and Shelby walked into the kitchen.

Addy cast her a sideways glance, then shook her head. "You're making a big mistake." Her eyes held more warning than animosity.

She didn't have to spell it out for Shelby to know who she was referring to. "Anyone watching Ryan can see how much he loves Chloe. He'd never do anything to hurt her."

"It's not Chloe I'm worried about."

Shelby shrugged. "Don't worry about me."

"I told you not to trust him, but you're not listening."

"I'm allowing him to protect Chloe. In the process, you and I are a lot safer, too."

Addy carried the bowl of vegetables over to

the table. "When you start falling in love with him, remember I warned you. He's left behind a whole string of broken hearts. He's the type that loses interest fast."

Down the hall, the water shut off and footsteps moved closer.

She lowered her voice to a whisper. "I'm not falling in love with him. I'm allowing him to protect his niece."

Ryan walked into the kitchen, still holding Chloe. His gaze moved from Shelby to Addy, then back again. Heat crept up Shelby's cheeks. If he'd overheard any of the conversation, she hoped he didn't think Addy's warnings were necessary.

Ryan smiled down at Chloe. "Show Aunt Shelby your clean hands."

Chloe raised them both, palms up. Her mouth curved in a tentative smile, those gold-green eyes a reflection of Shelby's own.

She wrapped her fingers around Chloe's tiny hands. "Good job. Let's put you in your high chair."

Chloe allowed Shelby to take her from Ryan, another hard-won accomplishment. As Shelby circled the table with the warm bundle in her arms, determination coursed through her. Nothing mattered but the little girl she held. Right now, Chloe needed protection. And Chloe came first. Addy would just have to deal with Ryan's presence and whatever scars their relationship had left on her heart.

As for herself, she was a long way from falling in love with Ryan McConnell. The warnings weren't needed. She was far too practical to be swayed by good looks and flattering words.

But if she was wrong, if she wasn't as impervious to Ryan's charms as she thought, she would deal with the fallout later.

Even if the fallout was the pieces of her own heart.

Ryan pulled out of the Wendy's parking lot, then exited the base, waving at the security guard. As he rounded the gentle curve on Charleston Boulevard, he glanced to the left, where part of Bremerton's mothball fleet awaited dismantling.

A few minutes later, he merged onto Washington 16. The route he was on made a big U, taking him south through Tacoma before heading northeast toward Snoqualmie and North Bend. The other option was taking the car-and-passenger ferry across the bay to Seattle. It was much more direct but wouldn't shave any time off the trip.

Saving time tonight would have been good. He'd had to work about two hours later than he'd planned. The upside was that traffic would be lighter than usual. The downside was that he'd arrive at Shelby's well after dark, even with daylight savings time having kicked in over the weekend.

He'd called Shelby some time ago and told her to eat without him. The double-bacon cheeseburger and fries he'd had before leaving base had tasted great. But the fast-food meal wasn't Shelby's cooking, or even Addy's. Now it sat heavy on his stomach. He should have gone with one of their salads.

He'd never been a fast-food junkie, even before his five years of marriage. After his divorce, he'd moved from his wife's cooking to healthy choices in already-prepared meals or making his own.

When he exited the interstate and drove into North Bend, the streets were almost deserted. He turned into the alley and stopped next to Shelby's Town Car. The glow from the lights on the back of the building spilled over the vehicles but didn't reach the railroad tracks or the trees beyond. Upstairs, light seeped out around the edges of the dining room and kitchen curtains.

He killed the engine and slid from the Equinox. A wind gust swept through the alley, stirring up a few leaves. The rest sat in sodden clumps. As he made his way toward the stairs, he shot Shelby a quick text, then pulled his jacket more tightly around him. An earlier rain had left the air chilly and damp.

At the top of the stairs, he raised his fist for his usual rhythmic knock. The door swung inward before he'd finished.

"You got my text."

"Yep." Shelby backed up to let him in. "I wouldn't have opened the door otherwise, even with your secret knock."

He twisted the dead bolt. "I think we should have a peephole installed." The dining-room window was far enough away for someone to press himself against the door and remain out of view. Even stepping up to the door to ask who was there wouldn't be a good idea.

Shelby nodded. "I hadn't considered it before, but I agree. I'll call someone tomorrow."

Ryan looked around the room. "Where is Chloe?"

"Addy's giving her a bath." She motioned toward the couch. "They should be done in a few minutes."

He stepped behind the coffee table. A small bowl sat on top, a spoon resting against its side. It was her nightly snack. Between dinner and bedtime, she always indulged in a bowl of ice cream. She had for the past four nights, anyway.

"Your ice cream is melting."

She gave him a smile. "Would you like a bowl?"

"A small one. Same kind you're having." It looked like butter pecan. From what he'd seen, she kept several options on hand. "I've had more ice cream in the past week than I've had all year. You're a bad influence on me."

"Everyone needs at least one vice. This is mine." She grinned. "And chamomile tea."

That was another habit he'd noticed. She always had a cup of tea before going to bed. He cocked his head sideways. "If it's healthy, it can't be a vice, right?"

"Maybe not." She flashed him another disarming smile. "I can make the same argument for the ice cream. It's made from milk, so it's a good source of calcium."

He returned her smile. "If you say so."

A few minutes later, both bowls were empty. Addy carried Chloe into the room and stood her on the floor. "Say night-night to Aunt Shelby."

Instead of going to Shelby, Chloe released a squeal and ran to him. "Wyan!"

Addy's features darkened. But Ryan didn't care what Addy thought. He gave Shelby a sideways glance.

She was smiling, green eyes sparkling with love for her niece. There was no jealousy, no pettiness. If Chloe was happy, Shelby was happy. Respect swelled inside him. How wrong had he pegged her at that first meeting? It wasn't the first time he'd asked himself the question.

He lifted Chloe onto his lap. She was dressed in gray flannel pajamas adorned with pink and blue cars, her diaper underneath. Addy had started potty training her a couple of weeks ago. She'd since put those attempts on hold. Little Chloe was experiencing enough adjustments without throwing potty training into the mix.

Ryan wrapped his arms around her, and she tilted her head sideways to rest it against his chest. As her thumb slid into her mouth, he began to sing "Hush, Little Baby," substituting his name for the word "Papa." He'd never had a great singing voice, but Chloe didn't care. And Addy and Shelby wouldn't judge. Well, Addy would, but he'd quit concerning himself with her opinion a long time ago.

He finished the song and glanced over to find Shelby's gaze on him. She was unguarded, emotion swimming in her eyes. The respect and admiration he saw stirred something deep inside him.

But there was longing, too. Was it longing for something she wanted now, or something she wished she'd had growing up?

Mia had told him about their childhood, stories that weren't always consistent. Which picture she painted seemed to depend on what emotion she was trying to evoke. When playing the victim, her dad was a tyrant, her mother detached. Other memories painted a different picture—a spoiled child who seemed to get whatever she wanted.

Something told him that if Shelby ever opened up, her story would be different from the world he'd glimpsed through Mia's eyes. How else could two girls raised in the same home turn out to be so different?

He pressed a kiss to the top of Chloe's head and passed her to the next lap. The little girl's arms went around Shelby's neck. "Nie-nie."

"Night-night, sweetie." Shelby dipped her head to kiss Chloe's cheek. Her hair, soft waves rather than curls and several shades darker than Chloe's, fell into the little girl's face.

Ryan smiled, joy swelling in his chest. There was no more contest, for either of them. He and Shelby were a team.

Addy reached for Chloe. "Okay, you got your hugs and kisses and a drink of water. Now it's bedtime."

She took her from Shelby and left the room.

Ryan spoke, his tone low. "She seems to be adjusting well."

"She is. She sometimes cries for her mother, but not as often as I expected." Shelby frowned. "I think she'd bonded with Addy more than Mia."

He nodded. "That would make sense. She was with Addy twenty-four seven."

A whimper came from down the hall. Soothing words from Addy followed.

Shelby's eyes locked with his. "I don't want her to forget."

"It's inevitable. At fifteen months, there's no way she'll remember."

"It just makes me sad." She blinked away a sudden moistness and dropped her gaze to her lap. "It's been a week, and I still keep thinking I'm going to wake up and realize this is a bad dream. I wish I'd had more time with her."

She heaved a sigh. It was filled with regret—words unsaid, emotions unexpressed, opportunities lost. "From the time Mia hit adolescence, she moved from one crisis to another. Most were manufactured, but she kept everyone close to her in a constant state of turmoil. For the past two years, caring for Aunt Bea and trying to keep the diner afloat have consumed my life. Too many times, I've felt if I had to deal with one more thing, I'd snap. Mia would have been that one more thing."

She entwined her fingers, steepling her thumbs. "When we reconnected at Aunt Bea's funeral, I knew it was time to work on that relationship. I never dreamed she only had two weeks left."

His chest squeezed in an unpalatable mixture of sadness and guilt. "I'm sorry." She'd been crushed under the weight of grief and regret, and he'd added to her pain with his own predetermined assumptions. "I judged you without knowing your situation, and I was wrong."

When she looked at him, her mouth curved upward in a sad half smile. Her eyes held forgiveness. "It's all right. During that first meeting, the judging was going in both directions. I immediately put you into the same mold as your father."

He matched her smile with one of his own. "So I guess we're even." He held out his right hand. "Friends?"

She accepted the handshake. "Friends."

*Good.* In the coming weeks, he'd keep reminding himself of that fact. They were friends. The problem was, the more he learned about Shelby, the more he admired her. She wasn't self-centered, like he'd initially thought. Just the opposite. She regularly set aside her own desires for the needs of others. She was ambitious and resourceful.

And she was beautiful. Her smile brightened the darkest room, canceling out Addy's negativity. When she hummed, the soft, sweet notes wove a path to his heart.

Addy returned and took her place on the

love seat. "Chloe's almost asleep, if she's not already. When I left the room, she was sucking her thumb and clutching her seal, eyes closed."

Ryan nodded. "Good. I assume there weren't any threats today." His question was for both of them.

Shelby's "nothing" came at the same time as Addy's "maybe."

Shelby looked at her sharply. "You didn't tell me."

"I wasn't sure, so I didn't want you to worry. Besides, the parking lot was full, so there were plenty of people in the diner. And I had the alarm set."

Shelby leaned forward. "What did you see?"

"A guy standing on the sidewalk across the street, down a little from where I saw the one who attacked Ryan. He was wearing a long raincoat with the hood pulled up, so I couldn't see his face, but he was the same size as the other guy."

Ryan tightened his hands into fists. "Why didn't you call the police?"

"And say what? That there's someone on the sidewalk in a raincoat? It was raining."

"You could have said he looked like the guy they'd chased the last week. They would have checked it out."

"He'd have been gone. He got away before, even with you chasing him."

Ryan sighed. She was probably right. "If you see anything suspicious, you should still call the police. But no one should look out windows, anyway." Whoever the guy was, he probably wouldn't fire into the apartment in broad daylight, but Ryan wasn't willing to take chances.

Shelby stood to carry their ice-cream dishes to the kitchen. When she returned, she propped both legs up on the coffee table. "Is everything still on for tomorrow?"

"Yep." They'd decided to do the DNA testing then. "I'm not reporting for duty until two in the afternoon."

Addy pulled a throw pillow into her lap and fiddled with its fringe. "You don't think Ryan's parents could win, do you?"

Shelby looked at him for the answer, even though the question was directed to her.

"We'll do everything in our power to make sure they don't." The thought of his father raising Chloe twisted his insides into knots.

Addy nodded. "Your lawyer needs to bring up Dorothy McConnell's mental condition."

He and Shelby spoke at the same time. "What mental condition?"

Addy shrugged. "That woman's got some serious issues."

"Since when?" There'd been nothing wrong with her when he left. Of course, that had been twenty years ago. Who knew what twenty years with his father had done?

"According to Mia, it happened when your sister and her little girl were killed."

Shelby's head swiveled toward him. "You lost a sister?"

He nodded. "A drunk driver crossed the median, hit them head on. Both Rachel and little Kaia were killed instantly."

It had happened almost two years ago, shortly before he arrived at Naval Base Kitsap. His father hadn't even bothered to get word to him so he could attend their funeral. Ryan had found out when he let Kyle know he was back in Washington and his friend offered his condolences.

Shelby put a hand over his. "I'm so sorry. I know how hard it is."

Yeah, she did. Her words weren't empty platitudes. He rolled his hand over and gave hers a grateful squeeze. A jolt passed through him, a link that went beyond their joined hands. Their shared grief connected them on a much deeper level.

When Shelby released him, he curled his fingers into a loose fist, trying to capture what he'd felt. It didn't work. The moment she let go of his hand, she seemed to take all the warmth with her.

He looked at Addy to continue. Her jaw was tight; her eyes narrowed. He ignored her displeasure.

Shelby did, too. "When your mom was here, I couldn't tell. I had no idea she had issues."

*Stepmom.* But Ryan didn't correct her.

"Recently," Addy said, "she's done better. Although Mia tried, she couldn't take Rachel's place. But Chloe helped fill the void left by Kaia's death. That's one reason the McConnells got so attached to her."

She put aside the pillow and crossed her arms. "They couldn't have been happy about Mia's decision to relocate to Arizona and move back in with her parents."

Shelby sat upright, her back ramrod-straight. "What?"

Addy shrugged again, lifting only one shoulder. "She was going to tell you when you guys went out to dinner."

"Why would she move in with Mom and Dad?"

Shelby's tone spoke volumes. Home wasn't a happy place. Maybe Mia's "victim" stories belonged to Shelby.

Addy continued. "Mia has been crazy about Randall as long as I've known her. But all he did was use her. Or worse yet, ignore her. She even tried to get into Robert and Dorothy's good graces, figuring that would be a roundabout way to Randall. She refused to give up, but then Randall got arrested. She wasn't willing to wait fifteen or twenty years for him to get out of jail."

Addy took a deep breath and let it out. "So she announced she was going to turn in her two-week notice, gather her belongings and move with Chloe to Arizona. I was fine with it. I don't have any ties, so starting a new adventure somewhere else sounded great to me. But when the McConnells found out, they couldn't have been happy."

Dread trickled over Ryan, filling every pore. No, they wouldn't have been happy. They'd have been devastated.

The blanket of dread grew heavier, threatening to smother him. Was it possible that sorrow over Rachel and Kaia's deaths drove his father to have Mia killed rather than let her leave with Chloe?

When he looked at Shelby, her face was pale, her eyes wide. Her thoughts were probably traveling the same dark path as his.

But everything within him objected. His father was capable of a lot of things. He had no doubt the man had killed before. Maybe not by his own hand, but he'd given the orders. More than once. If Mia had obtained evidence that could put him behind bars, he'd do whatever he could to keep it hidden.

But snuffing out a young woman's life in order to take her child entered a whole new realm of cruelty.

# FIVE

"That was easier than I expected."

Shelby walked toward Ryan's Equinox carrying Chloe, the building that housed ARCpoint Labs behind them.

Ryan nodded. "I'd envisioned needles and lots of tears."

"Me, too." But now DNA testing involved a simple saliva test, swabbing the inside of the cheek with what looked like a Q-tip.

After getting the subpoena two days ago, Shelby had done some research. The Seattle area had several options for labs. She'd decided to use ARCpoint because of its glowing reviews. She'd made a good choice.

Ryan pressed the key fob and the locks clicked. After buckling Chloe into her car seat, Shelby slid into the front.

Ryan started the engine. "Are you in a hurry to get back to the diner?"

"Not especially." Tessa and the other ladies would have everything under control. "Why?"

"What do you say we stop for an early lunch in Bellevue?"

"Sounds good." Not because she was hungry. They'd had breakfast at the diner right before leaving for Seattle. But the idea of lunch away was too appealing to resist.

During the week since she'd brought Chloe home, she hadn't gone anywhere except the bank and grocery store. Ryan had put a stop to even that after he was attacked last Thursday night, insisting she not go anywhere without him.

She had to agree. No sense making herself a target more than she already was. But she was getting antsy. She lived in one of the most beautiful areas of the country and couldn't even get out to enjoy it.

No matter how busy she'd been, she'd always managed to carve out time to be in nature. It was how she recharged. Even sitting for fifteen minutes in the park downtown calmed her thoughts and lifted her spirits.

As Ryan guided his vehicle up the ramp to I-90, Shelby twisted to look at Chloe in the backseat. She was sitting quietly, clutching her stuffed seal. They'd brought it into the lab, planning to try to distract her from anything frightening or unpleasant. They hadn't even needed it.

Shelby straightened in her seat. "I'm glad we're not going right back to North Bend. Getting out has been good for Chloe. Other than a handful of trips down to the diner, she's been cooped up in the apartment since I brought her home."

Ryan nodded. "I know it's hard."

The seriousness in his tone pulled her gaze to his face. Something told her he wasn't just talking about Chloe. For the second time, he'd seen past the surface to know what she was feeling. With that sensitivity, in addition to his good looks, it was no wonder women lost their heads and hearts around him.

Addy had said he was a ladies' man. So far, Shelby had seen several sides of him—determined opponent, loving uncle, vigilant protector. But she hadn't seen the Ryan that Addy described.

Of course, he wouldn't have any reason to show her that side of him. He likely had his pick of exotic, drop-dead gorgeous women, like those who worked in his father's clubs.

Women like Mia and Addy.

She drew in a deep breath. "Yeah, getting away has been good for me, too."

As she stared out the window, she let her gaze

slide along the horizon. It was one of those rare clear days without a drop of rain in the forecast and visibility that stretched into the surrounding counties. Mountains rose all around, their craggy forms topped in white, sunshine spilling over their rocky slopes. To the south, one towered high above the others.

She smiled. "We picked the perfect day. Mount Rainier is even out." As she said the words, pain stabbed through her. Aunt Bea loved the times when rain, mist and clouds didn't obscure the scenery.

Shelby always missed her aunt, but some moments were worse than others. Like standing alone in the diner before anyone else arrived, as remnants of conversations echoed through her mind. Or driving past her aunt's church, where Aunt Bea had proudly showed off Shelby to her friends, saying she'd never make it without her niece.

Even the things that hit her out of the blue, like when she'd pass Aunt Bea's favorite flavored coffee in Safeway and be slapped with the image of her aunt sitting at the table in the apartment, hands wrapped around her steaming mug, Bible open in front of her.

"What do you think of Applebee's?" Ryan's words cut into her thoughts.

"Sounds good."

Ryan exited in Bellevue, where the restaurant was right off the interstate. After he'd pulled into a space, she glanced around the parking lot. Ryan did, too.

It wasn't necessary. No one knew where they'd gone. Dave Jenkins had stopped at the diner for coffee, then insisted on following them in his cruiser. He hadn't turned back until he'd trailed them some distance up I-90.

Inside the restaurant, the hostess seated them immediately. At eleven in the morning, more than half of the tables were empty. A young boy sat in a booster seat at the table next to them, a plate of chicken tenders and fries in front of him. He looked to be a little older than Chloe. The adults with him were obviously a couple. They had that glow about them, that I'm-in-love sentiment radiating from them every time they looked at each other.

After the server left with their drink orders, Shelby opened her menu to search for something for Chloe. It was her first time ordering from the child's menu. Over the next few weeks, she was going to experience a lot of firsts.

She settled on a grilled cheese sandwich and ordered a chicken Caesar salad for herself. When she finished, Chloe was twisted in her high chair, watching the little boy. Shelby followed her gaze.

The three people at the next table formed the perfect image of a happy family.

For several moments, she let her gaze linger. That happy-family concept had never been a part of her childhood, even on holidays. Her father ruled the home with an iron fist, critical of everyone, and her mother spent most of her days incapacitated with depression and anxiety.

And Mia had been thinking about moving back in with them.

"You look like you're deep in thought."

She shook her head. "I'm still trying to come to terms with the fact that Mia had decided to live with our parents."

But it was true. Shelby had phoned them last night before going to bed, and her mother had confirmed what Addy had said. Mia had called two days before she was killed to say she was moving to Arizona and bringing Chloe with her. Her mother hadn't mentioned it at Mia's funeral. Of course, she'd hardly said a handful of words. She'd been almost catatonic, likely on some serious tranquilizers and antidepressants.

Ryan leaned forward, forearms resting on the table. "Maybe when she gave up on having a life with my brother, she figured she'd be better off going somewhere else, making a fresh start."

"If I wanted to make a new start, the last thing I'd do is move in with my parents."

"You sound pretty adamant."

"I am." She heaved a sigh. "I don't mean to make it sound horrible. A lot of people had it way worse than I did. My parents weren't abusive. Not physically, anyway."

The server approached with two glasses of tea and a small carton of milk. Ryan opened the top, then helped hold it while Chloe took some sips.

When his eyes met Shelby's, they held understanding. "Emotional and mental abuse can be just as bad."

She shrugged. "Even that makes it sound worse than it was." She didn't want him to think she was broken or something. "I just didn't have a normal childhood. As long as I can remember, my mom suffered with debilitating depression, so my older sister pretty much raised me." Shelby frowned. "As a kid, I was sure she hated me. Now I know she resented being tied down and took that frustration out on me."

"What about your dad?"

"He was just hard on everybody." Except Mia.

Each of them responded differently. Shelby tried that much harder. Lauren lashed out in anger. And their mom gave up rather than facing what she perceived as her own failures.

"You know how with some people, no matter what you do and how hard you try, you should have somehow done better?"

"I've met some of those."

She nodded. "That's my dad. Anyhow, Lauren escaped at eighteen, and from then on, I took care of myself and Mia."

"How old were you?"

"Twelve."

"That's a lot of responsibility to place on a twelve-year-old."

She shrugged. She didn't want pity any more than she wanted him to think she was broken. "It helped shape me into a responsible adult."

Their meals arrived, and she steered the conversation toward lighter topics. What had possessed her to spill all that to Ryan, anyway? She was usually more guarded than that. But his way of looking into her soul made anything less than full honesty seem pointless.

When they left the restaurant, it wasn't even noon yet. Ryan would have plenty of time to take her home and make it back to the base before two.

"Thank you for lunch." He'd insisted on paying in spite of her objections.

He shifted Chloe to his other hip to retrieve his keys. "It's the least I could do. If it weren't for my father, you wouldn't have had to go out. Besides, I enjoyed it. It was nice getting to know you better."

The smile he gave her sent a quiver through

her insides. She silently scolded herself. Of course, he'd want to know her better. They'd be co-parenting their niece for the next seventeen years—hopefully.

She watched him strap Chloe into her car seat. "I enjoyed it, too. My dinner with Mia and Chloe was going to be my first time out in about six months, unless you count doctor's appointments."

He closed the door and straightened. "Your aunt."

She nodded. During both of her times in North Bend, her life had revolved around Aunt Bea. As a result, she had dozens of acquaintances but no close friends.

She slid into the passenger seat and watched him take his place behind the wheel. "I'm not complaining. I wouldn't trade one moment with her for all the activities in the world."

"It sounds like you guys were close."

"We were. I spent a lot of weekends with her. Sometimes Lauren and Mia came, too, but usually it was just me. Mia was too young to hang around the diner, and Lauren was pretty busy with school and chores. Once Lauren left home, I didn't get to go as often. But those earlier visits had already shaped my future. At least they helped cancel out some of the damage that living with my dad had done."

He pulled from the parking lot and made his way toward the I-90 ramp. "I had someone in my life like that, too—my best friend's father. Weekends with my mom, I always got together with Kyle. My dad forbade the friendship. He was afraid the Gordon family would be a bad influence on me, like I'd go renegade and join the military or something."

She laughed. "Fortunately for you, his fears were realized."

"Yeah. Mr. Gordon is the reason I ended up enlisting instead of working in my dad's clubs." He accelerated up the ramp and merged with traffic. "So tell me about your aunt."

She pursed her lips. "I've told you a lot about me. Now it's your turn."

"Mom and Dad divorced when I was seven. He married Dorothy three years later."

"So she's your stepmother."

He nodded. "A few months after that, my dad started exposing me to the family business."

Her mouth dropped. "He took a ten-or eleven-year-old to his clubs?"

"Not while they were open. But he did include me in some of his meetings. As far as everything I've done with the Navy, it's either boring or classified." He grinned. "So tell me about your aunt."

She heaved a sigh. Their sharing was definitely lopsided. But she could talk about Aunt Bea forever. "She was amazing. Everyone loved her. No matter who she ran into, she always had a kind and encouraging word."

"She sounds like an awesome lady."

"She was. We both loved nature, so we did a lot of hiking while she still had the strength. Over the years, we've hit all the famous trails around here—Rattlesnake Ledge, Mailbox Peak, Kamikaze Falls, Mount Si, you name it." She glanced over at him. "Do you enjoy hiking?" She hoped so. It was an activity she planned to do with Chloe when she got old enough.

"I do. Kyle and I did it a lot when we were teenagers and when I would come back here on leave. Until we both got married."

*Married?* He wasn't still married, or he'd have mentioned it. Based on what Addy had said, it was hard to imagine any woman succeeding in getting a ring on his finger.

Ryan continued. "Kyle's wife loved strenuous outdoor activities, but mine hated them. And she didn't want me doing anything that took me away from her, which is understandable. Being married to a military guy isn't easy."

"How long were you married?"

"Five years. In the six years since we split, I've gotten back into hiking. Fortunately, Kyle's wife and I get along well, so she doesn't mind me tagging along."

"Maybe we can make it a foursome. Or a fivesome." Sadness settled over her. "Aunt Bea would have loved to introduce Chloe to the trails around here. Hiking was one of her favorite activities. She always said that being up on a mountain made her feel closer to God."

"What about you?"

She gave him a rueful smile. "It made me feel closer to my aunt."

"I thought you were a church girl. When we first met, you talked about taking Chloe to church."

"I didn't say *my* church. I said my aunt's." She frowned over at him. "So are you going to judge me now?"

Though he'd apologized, his initial condemnation was still fresh in her mind. So was the feeling of inferiority it had dredged up. All through her childhood, nothing she'd done was ever good enough. She wasn't smart like Lauren or pretty like Mia. Driving herself to succeed had boosted her flagging self-esteem but never brought the approval she'd craved from her father.

As an adult, she liked to think she'd overcome all that. She had, except for those rare occasions when she faced circumstances like this. Or perfect people like Ryan.

One side of his mouth lifted in a wry smile. "'Judge not, lest ye be not judged.' If I judged you for your lack of church attendance, someone would have to judge me."

So Ryan's promise to take Chloe to church was the same as hers—starting something new rather than continuing a long-held habit. For the time being, neither of them had to follow through with their words. Chloe wasn't leaving the safety of the apartment.

Ryan took the North Bend exit, then navigated the turnabout. When he pulled into the alley, Barry's Challenger sat next to the Camaro. Addy had apparently taken Shelby's advice and invited him over. Hopefully she'd had a good enough time to not still be miffed.

Shelby stepped from the SUV and opened the back door. Chloe's eyes were closed, her mouth slack. The seal was lying in her lap, one of her arms resting across it.

She unclipped the straps and lifted the little girl as gently as possible. Chloe stirred, then lay her head against Shelby's shoulder with a soft sigh.

Ryan stepped up next to her. "I'll see you safely inside."

"Thanks." At the bottom of the stairs, she

shifted Chloe to one hip and gripped the handrail. When she was halfway to the top, a breeze lifted a sheet of paper that was affixed to the door. Her chest tightened.

"Someone was here." Ryan's voice came from right behind her.

A sense of vulnerability swept through her, and she scanned the area. The only vehicles at that end of the alley were hers, Ryan's, Addy's and Barry's. From her vantage point several feet above the ground, she could see down the alley and railroad tracks a good distance in both directions. No one was loitering nearby. Unless someone was watching them from the woods.

When she glanced back at Ryan, tension emanated from him. He was wearing a light windbreaker-type jacket. Did he have his weapon underneath?

He nodded toward the door. "Get Chloe into the apartment."

She stepped onto the landing and jammed the key into the lock, casting uneasy glances at the paper. It was a single page, folded in half, "Shelby" printed across the front. Whatever message the sheet contained was hidden inside.

Maybe someone had tried to make a delivery and couldn't get Addy to the door. Shelby had contacted a handyman to install the peephole, but it wouldn't happen until this afternoon. So

Addy would have had no way of checking who was there.

No, if the visitor was a delivery person, they would have taken the package to the diner and had someone sign for it there.

When Shelby swung open the door, a high-pitched tone prompted her to enter her code. Addy had armed the alarm. Even though Chloe wasn't there, it was a good habit to get into. Ryan closed the door behind her, still outside.

Addy swiveled her head. "Everything okay?"

She was on the couch, Barry next to her. He had one arm draped around her shoulders. She'd apparently gotten over her annoyance with him.

"There's a sheet of paper taped to the door. You guys didn't hear anything, did you?"

Addy shook her head.

Barry twisted to face Shelby more fully. "There was something taped to the door when I got here."

"You didn't mention it." Addy's eyes held accusation.

Barry held up both hands. "It had Shelby's name on it. I don't mess with people's mail or personal messages."

Before Addy could respond, the door swung open, and Ryan stepped inside. "Call the police."

Shelby tensed at the urgency in his tone. "Did you read it?"

"I lifted it by one corner."

"What does it say?"

"Paraphrasing? He's watching. Knows what time we left this morning. Saw Dave follow us out."

Shelby began to pace. "What's that telling us that we don't already know? Addy has seen him twice. You chased him."

"There's more. He said someday, there'll be no one here to protect you."

His jaw tightened, the muscles working in the side of his face.

"And Chloe might become collateral damage."

Ryan opened his eyes, then pushed himself into a seated position, stifling a groan.

He'd always been a restless sleeper, shifting positions throughout the night. Since Shelby's couch was a little less than six feet long and he was an inch over, the flat-on-his-back position was out. So he slept on his right side, legs bent, spine against the cushioned back of the couch. Every morning, he woke up stiff, his shoulder aching and his back muscles tight.

But he'd sleep on a tile floor without a sleeping bag if it meant keeping Shelby and Chloe safe.

The investigation of Wednesday's note had

led nowhere. The security footage had shown someone climb the stairs wearing a ski mask, a bulky jacket and a pair of gloves, affix the paper to the door and hurry back down. Twelve minutes later, Barry had arrived.

No one in the diner had noticed anything. Other than two small frosted windows in the diner's kitchen, the only windows facing the alley were in the kitchen and dining room upstairs. Addy had been reading to Chloe at the time, sitting on the couch with her back to the door, so she hadn't seen anything, either.

Evidence was nonexistent—no prints and nothing distinctive about the handwriting. The note was written in block letters, all caps, using a fine-tipped Sharpie.

Ryan rose and crossed the room to peer out the front window. The sun wasn't up yet. But the streetlights, aided by a half-moon, reflected off a blanket of white. Wednesday they'd enjoyed a day of beautiful weather. Yesterday they'd paid for it with rain that began before lunch and continued through the rest of the day. By evening, it had turned to snow. Now it was Friday, and the temperature was a good twenty degrees colder than it had been just forty-eight hours ago.

He padded carefully toward the bathroom, the only sound the creaking of the wood floors.

Since he had to report for duty at seven, he'd have to leave well before daybreak. He'd showered last night, hoping to slip out this morning without disturbing anyone.

After dressing in his camouflage uniform and slipping on the matching cap, he programmed the Keurig for a single cup and took a box of granola from the pantry. The coffee was Shelby's. The cereal was his, along with the walnuts and banana he added. So far, he'd stopped twice for groceries. Both times Shelby had tried to pay him. Both times he'd told her they'd settle up later. He'd delay "later" as long as possible.

Shelby hadn't hinted at her financial position, but it had to be shaky. When he'd mentioned life insurance, she'd told him Mia hadn't had any. He'd never had to pay for a funeral, but he knew they weren't cheap. Neither were security systems. Or lawyers. Unless she had a nice nest egg accumulated, she had to be hurting.

After pouring a liberal amount of milk over his cereal, then doctoring his coffee with cream, he sat at the kitchen table. Down the hall, a door creaked open.

Great. If it was Addy he'd disturbed, he'd never hear the end of it.

He plunged the utensil into the bowl and brought a generous spoonful to his mouth. If he'd awoken Addy, she'd just have to deal with it. A minimal amount of noise in the morning was a small price to pay for the security he provided.

But it wasn't Addy who appeared in the doorway a half minute later. Shelby drew to a sudden stop, eyebrows lifting behind a stray curl that had fallen into her face.

"You're still here." She ran her fingers through her hair, and a flush crept up her cheeks, as though she'd become suddenly conscious of her appearance.

She had nothing to worry about. She was cute. Her eyes were sleepy, half-shielded by fringed lids. Mussed curls flowed down each side of her face and tumbled over her shoulders.

She moved closer, the legs of her lavender flannel pajamas slightly too long. With each step, they brushed against the floor with a soft *shhh*. Her toes peeked out, the nails painted a sparkly shade of copper.

"Sorry I woke you."

"Better me than Addy." She grinned. "I think she'd just as soon shoot you as look at you."

That was an understatement. Her hatred was almost palpable. Now he was getting it from two directions. Yesterday, Barry had stopped in for another visit, and several times, Ryan had caught the man staring, eyes narrowed. Barry's animosity made no sense, but he knew the source of Addy's.

"You know what they say about a woman scorned."

"Uh-huh." She nodded in that way women do when they have inside information. Or think they do.

"Addy's a major flirt, and she's not used to being turned down. When she tried it with me, I let her know right away I wasn't interested." He spooned some cereal into his mouth.

"Really?"

"You seem surprised."

She shrugged. "I'd assumed she was one of your conquests who didn't handle it well when it was time to move on."

One of his conquests? Where had that come from? "Addy and I never had a relationship. She's not my type."

"Who *is* your type?"

The way she snapped her mouth closed told him she wished she could unask the question that had just slipped out.

He took another bite, chewing slowly. Who was his type? Someone sensitive, unselfish, caring. Someone ambitious but willing to give of herself, strong but flexible enough to adapt to whatever life threw her way.

He'd just mentally described Shelby.

He stabbed the spoon into what was left of his cereal and turned over the contents, stirring them together. The first time he'd learned that Dana had cheated on him, he'd been deployed. For several days, he'd stumbled around in a daze, sure he was going to wake up at any moment and learn it was all a bad dream.

The second time…yeah, he was idiot. He'd taken her back, unable to resist the tears and pleas and apologies. The second time should have been easier. It wasn't. For months, he'd alternated between wanting to put his fist through something and longing to curl into a fetal position until the pain and anger and self-reproach dissipated. Six years later, the memories still had the power to rattle his world.

He met her gaze. "No one." No one at all.

She broke eye contact. "The snow has stopped."

"You looked out the window?"

"A quick peek through the miniblind slats."

Yeah, the bedrooms had blinds behind the curtains, the only rooms in the apartment that did. But he still didn't like it. "You need to be careful."

She rested her elbows on the table, fingers entwined. "If someone wanted to shoot me through the window, they'd do it while I'm in the diner."

The diner windows had blinds, but during business hours, they were always open. And though Shelby had agreed to remain in the back as much as possible, she still had to interact with her customers.

If his dad was the one behind the threats, firing into a crowded diner wasn't his style. He'd figure out a way to do it that didn't involve other people, despite the threat in the note. Robert McConnell's attacks were always focused. His guys were good at what they did.

As he spooned the last bite of cereal into his mouth, Shelby glanced at the digital clock on the stove, then reached for his empty bowl. "I've got this. You need to get going. With the snow, it'll take longer."

"Thanks."

She walked with him to the door, where he punched in the code to disarm the alarm. She'd given it to him last night, knowing he'd be heading out early.

"Drive carefully."

"I will." As he twisted the knob, bittersweet memories punched him in the gut. Enjoying conversation over breakfast instead of staring at an empty chair. Acknowledging the wish for a good day, rather than leaving a silent, empty apartment. Getting that hug and kiss goodbye.

Even during those times Dana was unfaithful, she'd always been good at pretending.

Instead of giving him a hug and kiss, Shelby wiggled upraised fingers. He waved back, then turned to go down the stairs. The door closed softly behind him, the dead bolt sliding into place a second later. He didn't have to caution her to lock the door and set the alarm. She was as safety-conscious as he was.

When he reached the ground, he scanned his surroundings. The soft glow of the exterior building lights spilled into the alley. Footprints marred the freshly-fallen snow. Someone had walked up the alley, disappeared between Addy's Camaro and Shelby's Town Car, then retraced their steps.

He approached, hand on his weapon. Addy's Camaro was covered with two inches of snow, Shelby's Town Car next to it. When he stepped between the vehicles, he skidded to a halt. A four-foot-by-two-foot area near the Town Car's wheel well had been wiped clean, as if someone had lain down, then moved closer.

Dread slid down his throat, lining his stomach with lead. Someone had tampered with Shelby's car.

He touched the flashlight app on his phone, then lowered himself to the ground at the front bumper. When he directed the beam toward each wheel, the brake lines looked intact. But a cylindrical object was attached to the frame on the driver's side. He scrambled to his feet and stumbled away, his legs threatening to collapse. He needed to call the police. But first, he had to alert Shelby.

If what he'd seen was a bomb, it was likely rigged to explode when she started the car or hit the brakes or accelerator. But if it detonated prematurely, it could wipe out the diner. He had to get everyone away from the building. He ran up the stairs two at a time and pounded on the door, shouting for Shelby to open it.

When she did, fear filled her eyes. "What—"

"Get Chloe and Addy. I think someone planted a bomb under your car. We've got to get out of here."

Her eyes grew even rounder, and her jaw went slack.

"Go. Now."

His command spurred her to action. She spun and disappeared down the hall as he dialed 911. Shelby's voice reached him, tinged with panic. Addy responded, sleep and confusion slurring her words. Soon Chloe began to cry.

As he finished with the dispatcher, Shelby hurried from the bedroom with Chloe wrapped in a blanket. "There's no time to get dressed."

She flung the words over her shoulder. "Grab a coat and shoes."

Shelby shoved Chloe into his arms, then ran back down the hall to disappear into her own room. A minute later, both women met him in the living room, boots accessorizing their pajamas. Shelby took two coats from the rack by the door, handed one to Addy, then returned to pull an afghan from the back of the couch.

After checking his own vehicle, he helped the women inside and drove a block away. The next task was notifying the base. He wouldn't make it in at seven. Maybe not at all.

By the time the King County bomb squad arrived with their explosives-detection canine, the police had everything in a one-block radius roped off with caution tape.

Addy leaned forward in the backseat. "We need to get Chloe away from North Bend. Let me take her."

Ryan frowned. "Not an option." For a lot of reasons.

"You need to quit being stubborn and think about what's best for Chloe."

He tamped down his annoyance, resisting the urge to boot Addy from the truck and make her wait outside. She was frustrated, like the rest of them. The feeling of helplessness was getting to them all.

"My parents' farm is safe. My dad has guns. So do his farm hands."

The thought of Addy driving Chloe there alone was scary, but the picture she painted was appealing—sprawling fields and pastures, view open for miles, two or three armed men at every building, a mini militia. And Chloe tucked away safely inside the house.

Of course, Addy could be exaggerating. Maybe that protection was nothing more than an old farmer with a .22 and a couple of guys with pellet guns. The truth was probably somewhere between.

But what waited in Idaho was irrelevant. "Custody hasn't been decided yet. Until the courts sort this out, no one can disappear with her."

He restarted the engine and put the heater on full blast. Over the next hour and a half, he repeated the action numerous times. With temperatures in the high thirties, the warmth was dissipating within minutes of turning off the truck.

Chloe started to cry again, and Addy tried to soothe her. "I think she's hungry."

Ryan checked the clock on the dash. "It's almost seven thirty. Let's head over to Twede's for some breakfast. My treat. It'll probably be a while before they let anyone cross the perimeter."

Shelby looked down at her flannel-covered legs. "Addy and I are in our pajamas."

"You look fine. Button your coat and no one will notice."

She gave him a get-real look and crossed her arms. She had a point. Twede's Cafe, featured in the TV series *Twin Peaks*, did pretty brisk business. She'd be sure to run into people she knew.

"Come on, Shelby. You had a bomb scare at five thirty in the morning. No one expects you to be dressed, makeup on and hair styled."

She heaved a sigh, worry settling into her features. "This story's going to spread from one end of town to the other by lunchtime." She let her head fall back against the seat. "I can handle being closed for the day. But what impact will it have on my future business?"

He reached across the console to squeeze her shoulder. "Don't you think your customers are loyal enough to return as soon as the caution tape comes down?"

She lifted her brows. "If you knew someone had a bomb planted at their business, would you patronize it?"

He winced. No matter how much people liked Shelby, if they believed affiliating with her would endanger them or their families, they'd go elsewhere.

Chloe cried louder, and Ryan put the Equinox into gear. Whether Shelby wanted to eat or not, he needed to get his niece fed. He pulled into Twede's parking lot a few minutes later. When the café opened at eight, they were the first ones in. The two women slid into one of the white vinyl booths opposite one another, and Ryan took his place next to Shelby. Chloe sat in a high chair at the end.

When their meals arrived, the little girl dug into her scrambled eggs and toast with gusto. Within twenty minutes, every morsel was gone. Addy and Shelby didn't do as well with their omelets. They could have shared a meal and still had leftovers.

Their conversation was as subdued as their eating. Finally, Addy rose from the table and walked to the restroom. Shelby stared past him to where people were lined up at the bar on chrome-and-red-vinyl stools.

"We'll get through this." He took her hand, which rested on the seat between them.

She entwined her fingers with his and squeezed, as if clinging to a lifeline. "How?"

"I don't know. But whatever happens, you won't be facing it alone. They'll catch whoever's doing this."

Her eyes met his, searching for assurances he didn't know how to give. "I've read everything I could find about your father. Police have watched him for years but haven't caught him in anything."

"This morning, he got careless, or someone did. He left tracks."

She pursed her lips. "Anyone who knows my routine knows I don't go out until after the diner closes. The snow would have melted by then."

Her gaze shifted, and he turned to see Addy walking toward them. Shelby gave a small tug of her hand. He held on a moment longer, then released her.

By the time they headed back to the diner, law-enforcement officials were removing the caution tape. Ryan waved down the bomb-squad vehicle as it moved through the parking lot, then jumped from the Equinox.

"What did you find?"

"Definitely a bomb, homemade, probably amateur."

"How was it supposed to detonate?"

"There's no timer, and it wasn't wired to the brakes or ignition system. Seems to have a tilt fuse."

"What's that?" During his twenty years with the Navy, he'd never dealt with munitions.

"Usually has a mercury switch. One end has the mercury, the other has two electrical contacts linked to a battery and bomb. When it's tilted, like with the hills around here, the mercury slides down the tube, closes the circuit and…ka-boom!"

Ryan flinched at the last word.

"We'll have more details in the next few days."

As the vehicle pulled onto North Bend Way, Ryan stared after it. The expert had said it was homemade. Amateur.

Nothing his father did was amateur. When he set out to kill someone, he succeeded. And his guys were in and out without a trace. His victims didn't know they'd been targeted until it was too late. If this was his father's people, heads were going to roll. Robert McConnell didn't tolerate mistakes.

The bomb-squad vehicle disappeared from view, and Ryan climbed back into the Equinox. Mia had said something was going on at the club and his father became the number-one suspect. But maybe they were looking in the wrong direction.

Whether it was his father, a patron of his club, or someone else entirely, it didn't matter. Someone had tried to kill Shelby.

Amateur or professional. Skilled or not.

Someone wanted her dead.

# SIX

The amazing harmonies of Pentatonix drifted through the diner, the volume a couple dozen decibels lower than usual. Today, it was Shelby's turn to pick the music. She'd chosen her favorite group. And her favorite CD. It didn't matter that it was their Christmas one and that Christmas was still nine months away.

She had reopened Saturday after Friday's bomb scare. Business had been slow, maybe one half to two thirds of normal. Yesterday, she'd been closed. Aunt Bea had insisted it wasn't right to do business on the Lord's day. Although Shelby didn't have those convictions, as long as she could afford it, she'd continue the tradition in honor of Aunt Bea.

She stuffed the cash she'd counted into the bank envelope and dropped it into the safe. Today was much better than she'd expected. Friday's excitement had passed, and it was almost business as usual.

When she walked from her office, a bucket rolled into the dining area from the hall that led to the bathrooms. Ryan followed, holding on to the mop standing up inside. His leave didn't officially start until Thursday, but he'd had today off. Over the past several hours, he'd been up and down the interior stairs so many times she'd lost count. She'd finally put him to work.

Once he was on leave, his constant presence would be a double-edged sword. Addy's grumpiness would be multiplied times ten.

But that wasn't Shelby's biggest concern. She'd been fighting her attraction toward him almost from the start. Every kindness he showed endeared him to her further. When he'd taken her hand at Twede's on Friday morning, she hadn't wanted to let go.

She needed him, as much for the emotional support he was giving her as for the protection. That was disturbing. She'd always been the one everyone leaned on, not the other way around.

Eventually, the threats would end. Ryan would go back to his routine, and she'd return to hers. And she'd have to shut off whatever feelings she developed for him. He'd always be there for Chloe, but Shelby wasn't part of the bargain.

When he'd said no woman was his type, he'd probably been thinking of his failed marriage.

It was something he obviously regretted. No wonder he ended his relationships before they could get too serious.

While he wrung out the mop and disposed of the dirty water, she made a final sweep of the kitchen. Everything looked good. Tessa met her in the doorway, raising her voice over the a cappella version of "Mary, Did You Know?"

"I think that's it."

"Excellent." She moved into her office and retrieved her keys.

There'd been no leads on who planted the bomb on her car. She'd been parked out of view of the camera at the back door. Ryan had made her remedy that. The Town Car was now in the lot right in line with the side camera. If anyone tampered with her vehicle again, the video would record the entire thing. Ryan and Addy had theirs parked in camera range also.

Shelby emerged from the office and killed the CD. Before she rounded the end of the counter, Ryan stopped her.

"I've got it." He snatched her keys and followed the three ladies to the door. After locking it behind them, he looked over his shoulder. "Code?"

"Zero-six-two-one." She heaved a sigh. "Can't we just hang a big banner outside that says, 'Mia didn't tell me anything'?"

"I wish it was that easy. I'm afraid this isn't going to be over until whoever killed Mia has gone to jail."

Her shoulders slumped. That was what she was afraid of, too. Tomorrow made two weeks since her sister's murder, and the authorities seemed no closer to solving it now than they'd been then.

Ryan set the alarm and followed her up the stairs. When they reached the living room, Addy sat next to Barry on the couch. According to Ryan, he'd shown up an hour ago. Chloe was up from her afternoon nap, sitting on Barry's lap. She was holding her seal, tipping its little flippers back and forth, a stream of syllables flowing from her mouth.

Addy had apparently passed her to him, and Barry didn't seem to know what to do with her. He was leaning forward, his back ramrod-straight. His pats on Chloe's back were stiff. He was a typical single guy. They were never comfortable around babies and toddlers.

Except Ryan. He interacted with his niece as if he'd been playing the father role forever. Of course, Ryan wasn't a typical single guy. He had a stability she'd never experienced growing up. And watching him with Chloe melted her heart.

The little girl looked up from her play, and a smile lit her face. "Be-be."

Shelby gasped, her heart rolling over in her chest. "Did you hear that? She just said my name."

Addy frowned. "I think she said, 'Be-be.'"

"She said, 'Shelby.'" She was sure of it. Chloe had looked right at her.

She danced over and swooped her niece off Barry's lap. After moving into the center of the room, she held her aloft and spun in two circles. "Yes, Aunt Shelby's home." She gave Chloe a noisy kiss on the cheek and held the little girl tightly against her chest. When her gaze met Ryan's, he was smiling, his eyes reflecting her joy.

After spending several more minutes with Chloe, Shelby handed her back to Addy. "I'm going to start dinner. Barry, are you staying?"

He looked at Addy before answering. At her slight nod, he smiled. "I'd love to."

Shelby walked into the kitchen, Ryan following. Happiness still coursed through her. She had overcome a huge obstacle. It wasn't just that Chloe had acknowledged her. It was the way she'd done it—the same way she greeted Ryan, the way a child reacts to a loved family member.

And Ryan was happy for her.

On sudden impulse, she spun and gave him an impromptu hug. "Chloe's adjusting to living with me. Not just adjusting, but flourishing."

She took a step back, letting her hands slide

to rest on his shoulders. "She's happy. And that makes me happy."

Ryan stood smiling down at her, his arms looped lightly around her waist. The admiration in his eyes touched her on a deeper level, stirring an unfulfilled desire she'd carried most of her life—the need for acceptance and approval.

But that wasn't the only way he was looking at her. His gaze also held warmth, as if he was seeing her as a woman. An attractive woman.

Goose bumps swept over her like a light caress. She leaned toward him, drawn by the same invisible force she'd fought for the past two weeks. It had been there from the moment she watched him step off the elevator at Mia's apartment. At first, it was an almost imperceptible tug. Since then, it had only grown stronger. Did he feel it, too?

He suddenly stiffened, dropped his arms and turned toward the counter. "I brought in your mail."

She cleared her throat, shaking off the effects of his closeness. "Thank you." She needed to get a grip.

She picked up the stack of envelopes and fingered through them, stopping when one caught her eye. "Did you know this was here?"

He cocked an eyebrow. "I bring it in. I don't snoop through it."

She tore open the envelope, knowing what was inside. The single sheet of paper was titled DNA Test Report. The columns of numbers meant nothing. The block underneath did.

Shock ricocheted through her body as realization slammed into her. She pulled out a chair and sank into it.

When she looked up at Ryan, concern etched his features. "What is it?"

She dropped her gaze to what she held and read aloud. "'Interpretation—combined paternity index, zero. Probability of paternity, zero percent. The alleged father is excluded as the biological father of the tested child.'"

She lifted her eyes to his face. "Randall isn't Chloe's father."

Ryan eased into the chair opposite her. His face had lost three shades of color.

Shelby shook her head, the ramifications sinking in. "Your parents have no right to her." She left the other conclusion unsaid. *You have no right to her.*

Ryan's attention shifted to a point over her shoulder, and she pivoted in her chair. Addy stood in the doorway, head tilted in silent question. She'd apparently passed off Chloe to Barry again.

Shelby indicated the paper she held. "Randall's not Chloe's father."

Addy's eyes widened and her mouth went slack. "I didn't see that coming." She leaned against the doorjamb. "Mia was always flirting with other guys, trying to get Randall's attention. She figured if she made him jealous, he'd realize he didn't want another man to have her."

Addy shook her head. "Apparently, she did more than flirt. I'm not surprised. Mia would stoop to any level to get what she wanted."

Shelby bit back the reprimand on the tip of her tongue. Addy and Mia had been best friends. And Mia was Shelby's sister. But what the other woman had said was probably true.

And that was just Addy. She had a critical streak wider than the Snoqualmie River. This wasn't the first time she'd bad-mouthed Mia. And she'd trashed Ryan on a number of occasions. When Shelby wasn't around, the woman probably disparaged her, too. Not the greatest example for Chloe. It was something Shelby would have to address in the future. Not now.

Addy pushed herself away from the doorjamb. "So Chloe doesn't have a drop of McConnell blood in her veins." Her lips twitched, as if she was stifling a smile.

Of course she'd be happy. The possibility of Robert and Dorothy McConnell getting custody of Chloe was now eliminated. Addy probably also thought she'd no longer have any dealings with Ryan. But Shelby hadn't decided yet how she was going to handle Ryan.

Chloe began to cry in the living room. Barry's voice followed seconds later. "Uh, Addy?"

Addy hurried over to rescue him. He didn't know what to do with a contented child. Holding a crying one probably sent waves of panic through him.

Moments later, Chloe stopped crying. Addy reappeared in the doorway with the child in her arms. "So what are you going to do?"

"I'm going ahead with getting legal custody, then pursuing adoption."

"What about him?" She tilted her head toward Ryan. "I know we need the protection now, but since he isn't going to be in Chloe's life long-term, it would be best for Chloe if he made a clean break as soon as possible."

When Shelby looked at Ryan, he appeared as if he'd taken a physical blow—a brass-knuckled punch to the gut or a knife to the heart. The last of the color had drained from his face, leaving behind anguish. It was painted into every pore.

"Shelby, please don't do this to me. Please don't do it to Chloe."

She watched as emotion contorted his features. Heard the plea to not shut him out of Chloe's life. Saw his eyes mist.

And she knew. Even though this test changed everything, it changed nothing.

She reached across the table to put her hand over his, which was clenched into a fist. "Chloe doesn't understand DNA. All she would know is that her Uncle Ryan, who has been in her life since day one, left her. Just like her mother did."

"So you're going to let me continue to see her?" The hope in his voice was mirrored in his eyes.

"I'm doing what's best for Chloe, and that's having you in her life."

Addy heaved a frustrated sigh. "That's not necessary. Kids are resilient. They get over things much more quickly than we do. Besides, it's better to do it now, while she's young, instead of waiting for the day he has his own family and moves on with a life that doesn't include her."

Shelby crossed her arms. "As long as Ryan wants to see his niece, my door will be open."

"She's not his niece." Addy turned to Ryan. "Chloe's not your responsibility. You're free of whatever obligations you thought you had."

Ryan's jaw tightened. "This has nothing to do with obligation or responsibility." He rose from the table and reached Addy in two large strides. She flinched but stood her ground.

"Love is a stronger bond than blood. I'm going to be an important part of Chloe's life as long as Shelby will let me."

When he tried to take Chloe from her, Addy resisted, not giving in until the little girl reached for him. Then she spun with a huff and stalked into the living room. A heavy silence permeated the apartment. Barry was keeping his opinions to himself. Smart guy.

Shelby rose and removed a large package of fresh salmon from the refrigerator. Dinner wasn't going to be pleasant. The food would be delicious. Her cooking was something she prided herself on. Aunt Bea had given her a great foundation. Then being responsible for her family's meals from age twelve forward had provided lots of experience.

But the company was going to be miserable. Addy would sulk, Ryan would stew and Barry would look as if he wanted to spring up and run from the apartment.

Maybe Barry and Addy would decide they'd rather have dinner out. Shelby wouldn't argue. She could think of a bunch of uses for leftover salmon. Besides, she had a lot of thinking to do, and she preferred to do it away from Addy's negativity.

Addy adored Chloe. It was obvious. For the past two weeks, that adoration had been a great comfort.

But now, Shelby had seen a different side of her. It was the first time Addy had allowed her own prejudices to supersede what was best for Chloe.

It had left Shelby questioning whether Addy was the best choice to provide the little girl's care. She would keep her on until Mia's murder investigation was closed. It wouldn't be fair to bring someone else into the situation. Addy knew the danger and had agreed to stay.

But once Mia's killer was caught, Shelby would reassess. If Addy wanted to stay, she'd have to let go of her bitterness toward Ryan.

If she didn't, Shelby would do what needed to be done. She had what it took to make the tough decisions.

Addy would have to go.

Ryan reached inside his darkened apartment to flip on the light switch. Today had been another long day at the base. Now, at almost seven in the evening, he'd prefer to head straight to Shelby's. But that wasn't an option if he wanted to wear clean clothes tomorrow. He also had a bunch of thirsty houseplants.

He swung the door shut, dropping the duffel

of dirty clothes onto the floor. First, he'd tend to his plants. He filled a gallon jug and walked to the wrought-iron stand against one of the patio doors. Orchids occupied the top shelf. Only one was in bloom, a tall stalk covered in delicate white flowers. African violets occupied the next shelf, frilly purple and pink blooms resting on fuzzy green leaves.

The bottom two shelves held a variety of plants—a Christmas cactus, two peace lilies, several bromeliads and a poinsettia someone had given him at Christmas. Above, two philodendrons hung from hooks in the ceiling, leaf-covered creepers trailing over the sides of the plastic containers.

He poured water into each of the pots and pinched off any dying leaves and blooms past their peak. It was nice not being the only living thing in the apartment. The plants weren't the company a cat or dog would be, but they also didn't require nearly as much care.

After he finished the watering chore, he grabbed the duffel and headed for his bedroom. Finding out last night that Chloe wasn't his niece had just about knocked him off his feet.

What he hadn't expected, though, was the sudden emptiness that had swamped him when he'd thought about never seeing Shelby again. No more listening to her hum while she worked. No more late-night conversations over ice cream. No more seeing the softness in her eyes as he caught her watching him with Chloe.

How had it happened? How had she gone from his adversary to someone he didn't want to live without in a little over two weeks?

Shelby intrigued him. She was the opposite of her shallow, flighty sister. She was also nothing like Addy, who was moody and unpredictable. Even with all she'd faced over the past month—losing both her aunt and her sister, the attempts on her life—she'd never taken out her frustrations on anyone else.

And she was beautiful, but unlike Mia and Addy, she didn't flaunt it. In fact, she seemed oblivious.

He unzipped his bag and, after dumping the dirty items into the clothes hamper, started repacking. If Addy had gotten her way, once the danger was over, he'd never see Chloe again. Her dislike for him wasn't any secret. But her antagonism had only gotten worse.

Last night's conversation with Shelby had given him some peace. She'd promised him he could see Chloe as long as he wanted to. If Shelby ever got tired of the animosity between him and Addy, Addy would likely be the one to go.

He selected some shirts and stuffed them into

the duffel. Maybe falling for Shelby wouldn't be a bad thing. If his feelings were returned, Chloe would be part of the package. Thirty-eight and divorced, he'd given up dreams of having a family of his own. But maybe that dream wasn't so far-fetched after all.

Yeah, it was. He shoved several pairs of socks into the bag, his movements jerky. Shelby was the same age as his ex-wife. If he couldn't hold on to Dana, how could he expect to keep the affections of an amazing woman like Shelby?

Besides, she didn't think of him like that. At first, she'd tolerated him for Chloe's sake. Since then, they'd fallen into an easy friendship. But he'd be crazy to hope for more.

The ringtone on his phone sounded, and his pulse kicked up several notches. But it wasn't Shelby calling. "Hey, Kyle."

Ryan and his best friend could go weeks without talking, but that never affected their friendship. Nor was it an indicator of how close they were. They'd each held the best-friend status since they met at age twelve. One called the other when he had something to say.

"I'm checking on you." Kyle's voice held more seriousness than usual.

Ryan had spoken with him shortly after Mia's murder to tell him what had happened and how it would affect him and Chloe. Of course, Kyle would have learned about it, anyway, if not by hearing it on the news, then in his capacity as a homicide detective with Seattle PD.

"How's it going?"

Ryan drew in a breath. "It's going. Chloe's been staying with her aunt, but I've been spending a lot of time over there."

"How is your niece handling it?"

Ryan didn't bother to correct him. Chloe would always be his niece, regardless of the results of some DNA test. Based on what Shelby had said, she would likely agree.

"She was crying for her mother at first, but she seems to be doing much better. I think it's because she has a nanny, and the nanny has stayed with her."

He pulled some jeans from a hanger and folded them in half, then in quarters, with one hand. "Are you involved in Mia's case at all?"

"It's not my case, but we all get briefed."

"What do you know?" He hoped they were closing in on his father. The man needed to come down for at least one of his crimes.

"I can't discuss an open investigation. You know that."

"How many years have we been friends?"

"Come on, Ryan. Your dad's one of our suspects."

"I've got a high-level security clearance with

the US government. I think I can be trusted to keep a secret."

"So what's the last piece of classified information you got?"

"What?"

"You heard me."

"Okay, point taken."

He propped his phone against one shoulder and wrestled the small stack of jeans into the duffel. "I'm going to let you go. I'm working on packing. After tomorrow, I've got three weeks of leave time and will be spending it at Shelby's. I'm sleeping on the couch."

He added the last detail knowing it would be important to his friend. The Gordons were a family who lived out their faith. Kyle had continued it in his own life, working as an assistant youth pastor.

Although Ryan had joined his friend for services several times as a teenager, his own attendance had been sporadic over the years. It wasn't that he didn't consider it important. It had always been something he was going to get serious about someday. "Someday" just hadn't gotten here yet.

"Enjoy your time off." Kyle's words drew Ryan's thoughts back. "Sounds like there might be a romance in the works."

"No, it's not like that."

Kyle probably wished it was. The two of them had married within weeks of each other. Kyle's marriage had lasted. Eleven years later, he was still crazy in love. Ryan was happy for him, but sometimes he envied him.

"I'm there because of the threats." Ryan didn't need to elaborate. Kyle and his fellow detectives would have been briefed on everything. "The bomb on Friday really gave us a scare."

It was a fertilizer bomb. He'd learned the details yesterday. Although it contained ammonium nitrate, the right compound, the fuel mix wasn't correct. Apparently, fertilizer bombs were harder to make than people realized. If the fertilizer and fuel weren't mixed in an exact ratio, the bomb wouldn't explode.

Two mistakes—leaving tracks in the snow and not getting the mix right. If that was his dad's man, he was doomed all the way around.

"Be careful." Kyle's tone held a heavy note of caution. "We're all working on it, both Seattle and North Bend. Or technically, Snoqualmie."

"Yeah." North Bend was too small to have its own department, so it contracted with Snoqualmie for police protection.

"Keep me posted."

"I will." He'd ask his friend to do the same, but it would be pointless.

Less than five minutes after ending the call,

he stepped onto the narrow front deck and locked the door. A full moon hung in a darkened sky, its glow spilling over the landscape, aiding the lights illuminating the parking areas. He jogged down the stairs to the first floor, then froze. His Equinox was sitting at an angle in its numbered space, the passenger side tilting downward.

He ran in front of the vehicle. When he reached the other side, his breath whooshed out. Both tires were flat, rims pressing the rubber against the asphalt.

Great. He had one spare, not two. Had he hit something? Run over some nails on the edge of the road? Or was the damage intentional?

He scanned the area. Lights were on in several of the surrounding apartments, but no one was outside. When he knelt beside the front tire, no nails or screws were visible. The same with the rear.

He opened the back of the SUV and removed the battery-operated compressor. After raising his hood and hooking the clamps to the battery, he pumped up the front tire. It inflated, but when he turned off the compressor and listened, he heard an almost imperceptible hiss.

As he moved his hand over the sidewall, a stream of air touched his palm. Using his phone's flashlight app, he found a half-inch slit.

Getting it plugged was out of the question. He'd need a new tire.

He carried the compressor to the back. When he'd pumped up that one, he turned off the machine and listened. Nothing. He checked the gauge and added another three pounds. After changing the front tire, he'd see if the rear one still had the recommended amount of pressure.

When he tested it twenty minutes later, it was still fully inflated. Apparently, someone had punctured the front tire and let the air out of the back. Why come all the way to Bremerton to tamper with his tires? Was it just to harass him?

No. It was to keep him from getting back to North Bend.

Leaving the compressor sitting in the driveway, he unclipped his phone and dialed Shelby. When she answered, his breath escaped in a relieved sigh. "Are you okay?"

"We're fine. Just finished dinner. We're getting ready to watch *Cars*. Why?"

"Someone slashed my tire." Or stabbed it. The slit was about the width of a small switchblade.

Shelby gasped. "Are you sure it was intentional?"

"Positive." He would think he'd hit something sharp and thrown it into the sidewall, but the air being let out of the rear tire blew that theory to smithereens. "I'm leaving now, but it'll take me an hour and a half to get there."

He ended the call and tossed the tire into the back of the vehicle, along with the compressor, jack and lug wrench. Fortunately, he had a full-size spare rather than a donut. He'd get the damaged tire fixed as soon as possible and hope he didn't have any other flats in the meantime.

After plugging his phone into the car's stereo system, he began the steep downhill grade toward Charleston Beach Road. In minutes, he'd be on 16, beginning his loop around the bay. He'd check on Shelby again en route. Maybe more than once. Someone obviously didn't want him there. The apartment was locked, but if an intruder barged in and triggered the alarm, minutes could pass before the police arrived.

As he approached Tacoma, brake lights lit up the road in front of him. He lifted his foot from the accelerator. It was almost eight o'clock, and the traffic heading into the city was moderate. Coming out, it would be much heavier.

He went for his own brake, then touched the screen to redial Shelby. Moments later, her "hello" came through the vehicle's speakers.

"You guys still all right?"

"We're fine. We've paused *Cars*, because Barry just arrived. Addy's letting him in now. How close are you?"

"Tacoma. About an hour, depending on what this traffic does.

"The movie will be over before then, but we'll keep Chloe up until—"

His pulse kicked into high gear. Why did she stop talking? "Shelby?"

"Hold on." A pause. "Barry asked who just left."

"What does he mean who—"

"Shh!"

He swallowed his question and waited. The voices in the background were too muffled to make out the words. Finally, Shelby continued.

"Someone was running down the stairs as Barry pulled into the alley. By the time he parked, the person had jumped the railroad tracks and run into the woods."

Ryan's stomach dropped. "Have Addy call the cops. And don't let Barry leave."

Tall and lanky, somewhat geeky and totally love-struck, Barry wasn't an intimidating figure. But his presence meant there was at least a man in the apartment.

Ryan kept Shelby on the phone until the police arrived. With every new traffic slowdown, his tension skyrocketed. When he finally pulled into the alley behind the diner, Dave Jenkins was heading to his patrol vehicle.

Ryan parked next to the dark SUV and hopped out. "What did you find?"

"Someone tried to get in. There were pry marks on the edge of the door and the door-jamb."

For the second time, his stomach did a free fall. If Barry hadn't arrived when he had and scared away the intruder, the creep might have gotten in.

"Anything show up on the video?"

"Someone entered the frame from the direction of the railroad tracks and climbed the stairs. But the pictures aren't much help. He was wearing a ski mask, a bulky jacket and gloves."

Ryan thanked him, then ran up the stairs. At the top, he banged on the door. "It's me, Ryan."

Moments later, it swung open, and Shelby stood there holding Chloe. Relief washed through him. He drew them both into his arms. As he pressed kisses to the top of Chloe's head, that sweet baby-girl scent wrapped around him, and a lump formed in his throat. If anything happened to his niece, he'd never recover.

And if anything happened to Shelby, he'd be just as devastated. He squeezed them more tightly and buried his face in Shelby's hair, breathing in an entirely different scent. It was more mature than his niece's sweet, fruity shampoo, but every bit as appealing—a citrusy, herbal hair product, maybe lemon and sage.

Longing curled deep in his core, an awareness of a void that had been there all along but he'd just now discovered. He'd convinced himself he was fulfilled, that his life was complete and satisfying. The brief periods of restlessness and the fleeting sense that something was missing had been easy to ignore. But now he knew. There was a Shelby-shaped hole in his heart.

He dropped his arms and stepped the rest of the way inside, closing the door behind him. In the living room, a movie was paused, a snaggle-toothed tow truck frozen on the screen. Addy sat next to Barry on the love seat, his arm around her.

Ryan's gaze shifted between Shelby and Addy. "Neither of you were watching the video feed?"

Shelby shook her head. "The iPad was on the couch next to Addy, but we were both focused on the movie. And we didn't hear anything over the soundtrack." She chewed her lower lip. "We can't watch it twenty-four seven, but we'll try to do better."

He nodded. Tomorrow he'd have to leave them to report for duty. One more day. Depending on Barry's class schedule, maybe he could hang out. If he was armed, even better.

He looked at Addy's friend. "Do you have a gun?"

Panic flashed in Barry's eyes. "Why?"

"Do you?"

"No. They make me totally uncomfortable."

Ryan held up a hand. "Chill. I'm not going to make you carry one. Will you be around tomorrow?"

"I can be in the afternoon. I have a class in the morning." According to Addy, he didn't have a job, just lived on his student loans. A master's-level engineering track was pretty grueling, even for someone with Barry's brains.

Ryan nodded. Better than nothing. The diner would be busy through the breakfast and lunch hours. By closing time, Barry would be here. And the police were patrolling on a regular basis.

Chloe pointed at the TV screen. *"Coz."*

Shelby smiled down at their niece. "You want to finish the movie?"

Ryan followed them into the living room and took a seat next to them on the couch. Shelby picked up the remote, and cartoon voices filled the room.

But Ryan's thoughts weren't on the dilemma facing Lightning McQueen. Images much more sinister circled through his mind—footage of a man, a ski mask hiding his face, a bulky jacket concealing his frame. A nameless, faceless threat.

Twice now they'd captured him on video. The first time, he'd left a note. This time he'd tried to break in, with Shelby, Chloe and Addy inside. Was he getting braver?

Or more desperate?

The man knew a security system protected the diner and apartment. Several windows held signs. But that hadn't deterred him. He'd apparently been confident he could get in, do what he'd come to do and get back out before the police arrived. The security system had meant nothing to him.

The creep's plans for Chloe were a mystery. But Ryan had no doubt what he wanted for Shelby.

He wanted her dead.

Ryan assumed the two goals were connected in some way but couldn't even say that for sure. If Mia had been killed for something she knew, what would that have to do with Chloe? If someone wanted to kidnap Chloe and hold her for ransom, why kill Mia?

He shook his head. The puzzle had too many missing pieces. He needed to find some answers. Soon.

Before the kidnappers succeeded.

Or a killer struck again.

# SEVEN

Steam rose from the grill, heavy with the scent of frying beef. Shelby stood with spatula in hand, ready to plop four sizzling burgers onto the toasted brioche buns waiting on porcelain plates.

During the years she'd worked with Aunt Bea, she'd worn every hat imaginable—server, hostess, cook, dishwasher and janitor. She'd even covered management-type duties like inventory, ordering and bookkeeping. It had prepared her well for the day she'd had to take over.

Jeri, Pam and Tessa were cross-trained also. They were her full-timers. There were two part-time people, too, women with elementary-school-aged children. They worked as servers and dashed out the door to meet the school bus as soon as the lunch shift was over.

Shelby removed the burgers from the grill, bubbling layers of melted Swiss cheese on half of them. The past couple of days, she'd been confined to the kitchen, at Ryan's insistence. With only two small windows, both frosted, it was the safest place in the diner.

She added sautéed mushrooms to the burgers with cheese and had just finished dressing the others with condiments when Pam swept into the kitchen.

The older woman eyed the four plates. "Frog sticks?"

Shelby nodded, and Pam moved to the fryer, with its basket of fries suspended over the top. Before she'd settled in North Bend five years earlier, Pam had lived a variety of places around the country, picking up regional diner slang at each place.

After Pam had walked away with the four plates on a large tray, Shelby peeled off the latex gloves and dropped them in the trash. The lunch rush was over, closing only twenty minutes away. She'd take the opportunity to run up and check on Chloe and Addy.

It would be her fourth time today. There hadn't been any scares. In fact, everything had been quiet since the incident last night. Addy was also keeping an eye on the video feed. If anyone headed up the stairs, she'd run down to the diner with Chloe and alert the police.

As Shelby walked from the kitchen, she wiped the back of her arm across her forehead, smearing what felt like a combination of sweat and grease. Tessa caught her at the bottom of the stairs.

"Just a heads-up, we've got an eight top. Mandy's taking their orders now then heading out. Gail already left."

Great. Twenty minutes until closing, and a party of eight walked in. But an extra eighty dollars in receipts? Yeah, she'd take it.

The diner phone jangled, and Shelby slipped behind the counter to answer it. When the caller identified herself as Dorothy McConnell, everything inside her tightened into a knot.

"I wanted to apologize for the things my husband said when we visited your place."

Sure, now that Shelby held all the cards, Mrs. McConnell was meek and apologetic.

The opinion unraveled even as the thought crossed her mind. Dorothy McConnell wasn't the one who'd threatened her. Robert was. She hadn't joined him. In fact, she'd seemed uncomfortable. She probably couldn't control her husband's actions any more than Shelby's mom could control her father's.

Not yet ready to accept the apology, Shelby remained silent.

The older woman released a small sigh. "I guess you know Chloe isn't Randall's child."

"I saw the report."

"That doesn't matter to us. She's our grand-child. We love her the same regardless of who her father is."

Shelby swallowed hard, trying to tame the nausea churning in her stomach. Was the woman going to ask if she could take Chloe? Or just visit her?

She wasn't comfortable with either. At first, she'd thought she would have no choice. Her lawyer had advised her that Washington recognized grandparent visitation rights. But Dorothy and Robert McConnell weren't Chloe's grand-parents, so they had no rights.

Silence stretched between them. Mrs. Mc-Connell seemed to be waiting for a response.

"What are you asking?"

"We want to be able to see Chloe, to take her places, let her spend the weekend with us."

A vise clamped down on Shelby's chest. No way would she let Chloe go into that home, even for a visit. Once Shelby gave permission, she might face a legal battle to get her back out.

"I'm going to be frank with you, Mrs. Mc-Connell. I don't trust your husband."

"He doesn't have to be involved." She spoke quickly, her tone pleading. "I won't bring her home. I'll take her to the park, out for ice cream, wherever you approve."

The vise squeezed harder. "I don't know. I—"

"You can even go with us. Please let me spend some time with her. I can't bear the thought of never seeing her again." Her voice broke on the last statement, shattering some of Shelby's resolve.

Mia had said the woman was unstable. She wasn't; she was just grief-stricken. And spending time with Chloe had helped ease a small part of her sadness. How could Shelby take that away from her?

Another image slid into her mind—her mother sitting at the kitchen table, staring out the window at flowers that didn't stir her, a well-manicured lawn she didn't appreciate, mountains she didn't see. From Shelby's earliest childhood memories, her mother had been a shell of a person, her mind numbed by antidepressants, mentally and emotionally disconnected from life.

Was that what Dorothy McConnell would become? How could Shelby go on with her daily activities, knowing she'd condemned the woman to the same prison cell her mother occupied?

"I need to think about it." And talk to Ryan. She'd get Addy's input, too. "But it's not safe for her to leave the apartment right now. There have been some threats."

"Against Chloe?" Panic had added shrillness to her voice. "What kind of threats?"

"The day after you guys left the apartment, someone tried to kidnap her."

"What? Oh, my word! You have someone guarding her, right?"

"I've had a security system installed, including surveillance cameras, and someone is with her twenty-four seven."

Mrs. McConnell released an audible sigh. If her husband was behind the attempted kidnapping, he'd apparently not let her in on it. That wouldn't make sense. If the man intended to have Chloe forcibly brought to their home, his wife would have to know. Maybe the person who'd attacked Addy and tried to take Chloe wasn't working for Robert McConnell.

Mrs. McConnell continued. "I'm glad someone is protecting her. Can I call you back tomorrow?"

"Okay." She'd talk to Addy this afternoon, then discuss it with Ryan tonight. Whatever happened, there was one thing she had to make clear. "If we agree to this, your husband isn't to know."

"I won't say a word. He doesn't even know I called you."

As Shelby hung up the phone, Pam walked toward the kitchen waving a handwritten meal order. "Jeri and I got this. You go check on your niece."

When Shelby reached the apartment, Addy was sitting on the couch, feet propped on the coffee table and a book in her hand. The iPad was next to her.

Addy looked up and smiled. "I just put Chloe down for her nap."

She laid the book on the coffee table, pages down and open. Judging from the muscle-bound guy on the cover, it was a romance novel.

Shelby shifted her gaze to the iPad. The screen was split into three sections. On the left half, wooden steps descended, the side of the building framing one edge. The rest of the frame displayed an angled section of the alley parking area visible over and through the railing. The upper right frame showed the view from the camera over the diner's entry door. Below it was a wide view of the parking lot. Any of the three pictures could be expanded to full-screen size with a touch.

Shelby nodded toward the couch. "You're keeping an eye on that?"

"You bet. I've had it with me the entire time, watching people come and go. Looks like the diner's doing pretty brisk business."

"It is. The bomb threat Friday doesn't seem to have scared away my customers." Shelby eased onto the couch.

Addy frowned at her. "You look like you have something on your mind."

"I got a phone call this afternoon."

"From who?"

"Ryan's stepmom."

Something flashed in Addy's eyes, the storm that was always brewing, ready to grow to gale force at the mention of Ryan's name. "What did she want?"

"She wants to see Chloe."

"Of course. You told her no, right?"

"I said I need to think about it."

"You're not serious." Addy twisted on the couch to face her more fully. "You should be thinking about getting a restraining order against them, not entertaining thoughts of letting them take Chloe."

"Not *them*. She would be seeing her alone. And she wouldn't be taking her anywhere. I'd be meeting them at a public place, giving her an opportunity to spend an hour or two with her granddaughter."

Addy's hands curled into fists and her jaw clenched. "Chloe isn't that woman's granddaughter."

"She may as well be. That's what everyone has believed for the last year and a half, including Chloe."

Addy sprang up from the couch and started

to pace. "That woman is way out there, and her husband is pure evil. He threatened you. These people tried to kidnap her. Or have you forgotten about that?"

"I haven't forgotten anything. But we don't even know for sure it was them. Maybe someone saw an opportunity for some easy money and figured they'd kidnap her and hold her for ransom. From what I've seen of Ryan's parents, they would have paid it." Shelby sighed. "I don't feel sorry for Ryan's dad, but I feel bad for his stepmom."

Addy stopped pacing to stare down at her. "You know what your problem is? You're too nice, not anything like your sister. Mia was for Mia and nobody else."

Shelby flinched at the venom behind Addy's words. But she couldn't argue with what she'd said. Mia had always been that way.

Shelby rose and headed toward the hall. "I'll discuss it with Ryan. But right now, it's a moot point. Chloe isn't leaving this apartment until whoever is threatening us is locked up and we know for sure she's safe."

Shelby swung open the door, pulled it shut behind her and started down the stairs. If Addy had a response, she didn't hear it.

The woman was getting awfully opinionated. She needed to understand she wasn't in charge.

Shelby and Ryan were. She'd always include him on decisions that affected their niece. Not because she had to, but because it was best for Chloe.

Maybe things would level out once the threats ended. The stress was getting to everyone—constantly being on guard, never knowing when a killer would strike again. No wonder Addy and Ryan were at each other's throats.

Addy was at Ryan's, anyway. Ryan seemed to let her animosity roll off him without feeling the need to engage. Shelby wasn't used to that in a guy. Too many she knew reacted at the slightest provocation. Too much testosterone and not enough self-control.

Her father reacted, but there was never any loss of control. He carefully selected every word, then aimed them to penetrate where they would do the most damage.

By the time Shelby returned to the diner, someone had turned the sign on the door to Closed, and the table of eight had just been served their meals. She'd never seen any of them before. Though North Bend wasn't a well-known vacation destination, it saw its share of tourists.

One other table was occupied. Old Mr. Brunner sat alone, a word search book in front of him, open but mostly forgotten. He was her most regular customer. According to Aunt Bea, he'd lost his wife six years ago, and afternoons at the diner and Sunday mornings at church constituted his social life. Most days, he walked in at eleven sharp with his pencil and word-search book, ordered lunch and didn't leave until Shelby brought out the CD player and whatever music she and the girls had planned for cleanup. She didn't begrudge him the time or the space.

Turning her back on Mr. Brunner, she moved into the kitchen to help with cleanup. Jeri carried in a tub of dirty dishes and laid it in the huge sink. After spraying the leftover food into the disposal, she arranged the items in the dishwasher. They wouldn't start cleaning out front until the party of eight left. Shelby would also hold off emptying the cash register until then.

The jangling of the phone overrode the clang of dishes and murmur of voices. Maybe Ryan was calling to let her know he was getting off early. When she picked up the phone, a McConnell was on the other end of the line, just not the one she'd hoped.

"What do you want?" She didn't try to inject politeness into her tone. If Robert had called to make threats, she would hang up on him.

"That's what I was going to ask you."

"I don't want anything from you."

"You might want to reconsider. That diner you own has a mortgage."

"One that'll be paid off in five years."

"It could be paid off next week."

What? Was he planning to pay her for visitation rights? "I'm not interested."

"How much did Mia's funeral set you back?"

"That's none of your business."

"Think what fifty thousand dollars would mean to you. One hundred thousand dollars."

The man was crazy. "I earn my money. I don't become obligated to anybody."

"There'd be no obligation. You could pay off everything you owe, take a fancy vacation and still have the start of a nice nest egg. Sign over your rights to Chloe. Let my wife and I adopt her. We'll even allow you to have visitation."

Her jaw dropped. "You must be insane."

"If you fight me on this, you're the one who's insane."

She snapped her mouth closed as shock gave way to anger. "Keep your money and your threats. My niece isn't for sale."

She slammed the receiver into the cradle, thankful she'd never replaced the old phone with a cordless. That action was much more satisfying than pushing a button.

As she backed away from the counter, both her hands shook. She'd just hung up on Robert

McConnell. From everything she'd gathered, no one told him no. And no one dismissed him. He'd probably killed people for less.

But in that moment, she was too furious to care.

Ryan lay on the couch, staring into the darkness. The soft glow that slanted in around the curtains didn't reach into the depths of the room. For the dozenth time in an hour, he flopped onto his back, knees bent, and folded his hands across his chest.

He wasn't the only one having trouble sleeping. Addy seemed to be as restless as he was. Although she'd been quiet, he'd heard her tiptoe out of the room she shared with Chloe several times. Once she'd made it as far as the kitchen, had a glass of water and then headed back to her room.

As soon as he'd arrived last night, Shelby had told him about the call from his father. The man had tried to buy Shelby's rights to her niece. Ryan should have been shocked. But he wasn't.

He couldn't remember a time when his father hadn't gotten what he wanted. When he had his mind set on something, he did whatever it took to get it, eliminating any obstacle that got in his way.

Addy had pressured them again to let her take

Chloe to Idaho. She was right that there was no more custody battle. But no strangers were going to provide protection for his niece when he could do it himself. Shelby had agreed with him. And Addy had almost blown a fuse.

Ryan shifted back onto his side, legs bent enough to plant his feet against the arm of the couch. He wasn't any more comfortable in that position than he'd been in the others.

After last night's argument, Addy had tried to storm out, but neither he nor Shelby would allow it. Other than the initial break-in, no one had targeted her. Even then, the intruder had been after Mia's phone and Chloe. Addy had simply gotten in the way.

But he wasn't about to let her venture out alone. If she got into trouble, he'd be faced with the difficult decision of leaving Chloe and Shelby unprotected or letting Addy fend for herself.

So Addy had snatched up her cell phone and stormed down the stairs into the diner. Since she didn't have the code to disarm the alarm, she hadn't been able to go any farther than that.

She'd probably called Barry and vented to him. She could vent all she wanted. She wasn't taking Chloe unless he and Shelby were in agreement with it.

Ryan pushed to his feet and paced the living room, the wood floor making soft creaking sounds. Pacing wouldn't help him fall asleep any more than tossing and turning had. But he couldn't lie there any longer. His muscles felt twitchy, like he was itching on the inside.

For the next three weeks, he was going to be living out of a suitcase. Or more specifically, two duffels. They both sat under the coffee table, out of the way but not hidden. There wasn't room for him to have his own space.

He stopped pacing. Someone stood where the hall met the living room. It was Addy.

She moved farther into the room. "You're still up."

He shrugged. "Having trouble getting to sleep."

"Me, too." She moved past the coffee table to sit on the love seat.

Ryan returned to his place on the couch, pushing the rumpled sheet out of the way. His weapon was tucked behind one of the couch cushions, handle accessible to him but not to anyone else. He waited for Addy to speak. He usually avoided being alone with her, but she didn't look like she was entertaining thoughts of flirting with him. She sat at the front edge of the cushion, back straight, hands clasped in her lap.

"Sorry I blew up on you guys. Everything's getting to me. I'm so worried about Chloe. I just want her to be safe."

Ryan nodded. He had to be dreaming. Addy hadn't been this civil to him since he'd turned down her advances. "Everyone's pretty stressed right now." He leaned against the back of the couch. "I'm guessing you called Barry."

"Yeah." Though it was too dark to see more than silhouettes, there was a smile in her tone. "He's good at talking me off the ledge."

Ryan lifted his brows. Usually Barry seemed nervous and uneasy, as if *he* was the one who needed to be talked off the ledge. Of course, Ryan only saw him when Addy was around. The guy probably stayed on pins and needles, terrified he'd make some blunder that would cause Addy to send him packing.

"Once this is over, I'll be fine."

While Addy had been downstairs allowing Barry to cool her down, Shelby had made a decision. Once the danger was over, she was putting Chloe in day care or finding a licensed person who cared for children in her home. Ryan had agreed.

Maybe they'd both renege on the decision. It would depend on whether Addy kept the promise she'd just made.

Addy stood. "Try to get some sleep."

"You, too."

After Addy walked away, he picked up Shelby's iPad from the coffee table. Three scenes displayed in varying shades of gray. Nothing moved in any of the views. Addy had wanted to keep it with her. She'd said that she'd been watching it all day and might as well continue.

Ryan had argued that since he was the one sleeping closest to the exterior door, he needed to be able to check the video feed the instant he heard a possible intruder. Shelby had agreed, and Addy had relented, without the temper tantrum.

After fluffing his pillow, he lay back down and pulled the sheet over him. With the T-shirt and nylon gym shorts he wore, and the thermostat set at sixty-eight, the light sheet was perfect. He closed his eyes and tried to quiet his thoughts.

Shelby had also talked to him about the conversation with his stepmother. He'd sided with Addy on that one. He didn't know whether she'd broken her promise and talked to his father, or whether his father had initiated the second call on his own.

But Ryan wasn't taking a chance. As long as Dorothy was married to his father, he wouldn't trust her with his niece.

A howl rose outside, then retreated as a wind gust swept through. A storm was moving in again. This one was supposed to bring only rain. Lots of it, accompanied by strong winds.

How fitting. The chaos outside would mirror the chaos within.

Eventually, the rain started, tapping against the roof in a soothing rhythm. His thoughts gradually grew random as sleep moved closer. Sound faded in and out. Then there was nothing.

His eyes snapped open. He was lying on his side, every muscle drawn taut.

The howls of the wind were much more intense, almost constant now. No longer a pitter-patter, the rain had become a roar. Was that what had awoken him, the ferocity of the storm?

He sat and snatched the iPad from the table. Movement drew his attention to the top right frame.

A raincoat-clad figure moved down the stairs, away from the camera, the vinyl hood covering the person's head. He clutched an object in his right hand, something thin and long. Maybe a demo tool, like a flat bar.

Something to pry the door with.

Ryan snatched his weapon and sprang to his feet, tossing the iPad back on the table. When he swung open the door, the alarm began to squeal and rain soaked him instantly. Squinting against nature's fury, he charged outside and stepped…into thin air.

He grabbed for the handrail, but the slick board slid through his grip. One shin slammed into something on the way down, and his weapon clattered to the asphalt.

His body came to a bone-jarring halt against two adjacent framing boards that had supported the floor of the landing.

A floor that was now missing.

As he hung suspended in the darkness, the assailant crossed the railroad tracks and disappeared into the woods. The squeal prompting the entry of the code changed to an ear-piercing siren. Now the system would notify the police.

He lowered himself the rest of the way through the four-foot-by-two-foot opening in the framing and dropped to the ground. His shin was screaming. So were his chest and the undersides of both upper arms, where he'd caught himself against the two-by-sixes. Next to him was a haphazard pile of deck boards.

He looked up, and the living-room light came on, illuminating the still open doorway. The landing light was off, the bulb likely unscrewed. Panic shot up his spine. Addy and Chloe wouldn't know about the missing deck boards. If either of them stepped out…

He limped toward the base of the stairs, waving his arms and shouting. But the alarm's wail and the howl of the wind swallowed his words. When he was halfway up, Shelby's head appeared in the open doorway. His heart stopped.

Her eyes dipped to what was left of the landing, then snapped to him. "Are you hurt?"

When he reached the top, he stepped on one of the framing members, then into the apartment, closing the door behind him. Without answering, he punched in the code and the alarm fell silent. Sirens sounded in the distance.

"Call 911 and tell them to look for someone in a raincoat. He ran into the woods. And when they come up to the apartment, watch for a missing landing."

After Shelby finished the call, her eyes swept him up and down. His T-shirt was soaked, and his gym shorts stuck to his legs, the fabric clingy and ice-cold. Rain dripped from him, joining what had accumulated while the door had been open.

"I've gotten water all over your hardwood floor."

"I don't care about the floor." Shelby's voice was higher-pitched than normal. "Are you hurt?"

"I'm okay." But now that the extra adrenaline was dissipating, everything was throbbing.

He looked past her to where Addy had entered the living room, her eyes droopy with sleep. She'd apparently gotten past her insomnia, too.

Shelby's voice drew his gaze back. "Your leg."

Her eyes had locked onto the part of his body that was screaming the loudest. Several inches of his left shin were scraped raw.

"It's just surface." Maybe. He'd likely bruised the bone. He must have instinctively jerked back his leg while falling or he'd have done serious damage to his kneecap.

Shelby dragged him toward the kitchen and pushed him into a chair. After pulling a clean towel from the drawer, she ran cold water over it. "Tell me what happened."

"The storm woke me up." Or maybe it was the distinctive sound of boards being pried up, the creaking of nails sliding through wood. "When I looked at the video feed, someone was walking away. I ran out and stepped right through the landing."

She dropped to her knees in front of him and touched the cool, wet towel to his shin. He winced, then relaxed, the pressure painful but the cold soothing at the same time. Or maybe it was her touch that he found so soothing.

She rose, then pulled a chair in front of him, positioning his foot on it, leg bent. She'd just finished filling a zippered plastic bag with crushed ice and wrapping it in another towel when a knock sounded on the side door.

She handed it to him and he held it against his leg. A few seconds after she disappeared, the door creaked open. When she returned to the kitchen, an officer followed her. His nameplate said Harris. Shelby had called him "Grady." As owner of a popular diner, she probably knew most of North Bend.

Buff and close to Shelby's age, he had dark hair, dark eyes and what looked like a killer tan. Considering it was March in Washington, the golden-brown skin tone was likely due to some Spanish blood rather than time in the sun, despite the English surname.

"Someone tampered with the landing and Ryan stepped through. He could have been seriously injured." The fire that lit her eyes warmed him inside.

Harris pulled up a chair. "Tell me what happened."

As Ryan relayed the events of the past fifteen minutes, the officer scrawled notes in his pad. He already knew about the other threats, including the bomb. Likely the whole department had been briefed.

When Ryan finished, Harris closed the pad and slipped it into his pocket. "We searched the area when we got the update, but didn't see anyone out and about. My partner's still looking around. With this downpour, there won't be any prints we can get."

He rose. "Looks like Shelby's taking good

care of you." He smiled down at her, his gaze warm. "She's a special lady."

Ryan nodded, something uncomfortable shooting through him. It felt a lot like jealousy. Where had that come from?

While Shelby walked Harris to the door, Ryan lifted his arms to study their undersides. The skin was already turning reddish purple, bruising that would likely get worse over the next few days.

After shutting the door, Shelby returned to the kitchen and whirled on him, eyes stony. "You need to leave."

"What?"

"Go back to your apartment."

He shook his head, trying to clear it. What did he do to tick off Shelby?

She planted both hands on her hips, staring him down. "I'm not going to see you hurt trying to protect me."

Now it made sense. "I'm not only protecting you. I'm also protecting my niece."

"Nobody's trying to kill Chloe."

He laid the wrapped bag of ice on the table and pushed himself to his feet, stifling a groan. Letting her tower over him while they argued put him at a disadvantage. "No, they're not trying to kill her, just kidnap her."

"We don't know that they're even trying to

do that anymore. Right now, he seems to be after just me."

"Which is precisely the reason I'm not going anywhere."

"Tonight's threat targeted you."

"How do you figure that?"

"Who was most likely to step out on that landing to investigate suspicious activity? Someone is upset that you're here and retaliated against you."

She had a point. But he wasn't willing to leave her unprotected any more than he was willing to leave Chloe.

She continued her tirade, slicing her hand through the air to emphasize her words. "I refuse to put you in the line of fire."

It was the first time he'd heard Shelby raise her voice. She stood before him in her lavender pajamas, hair a riotous mass of auburn waves, eyes flashing.

And he wanted nothing more than to kiss her. The urge swept over him with the force of a tsunami but with a lot less warning. He needed to get a grip before he did something stupid. Over the past half hour, his emotions had been all over the spectrum—panic as he fell through the landing, anger watching Shelby's enemy escape yet again, helplessness at not being able to stop him.

Or maybe it the way the cop had looked at her that had him teetering at the edge of his control. The man had eyed her with warmth and appreciation, the way a man admires a beautiful woman.

What did it matter? Ryan had no claims on her. He didn't plan to in the future, either. There was no reason for it to bother him. But it did.

He crossed his arms, the action infusing him with strength. His number one priority was protecting her and Chloe. He wasn't going to let errant emotions distract him. "I'm staying." His tone was low, determination giving it a hard edge. "Unless you intend to file a restraining order against me, you're going to have to put up with me for the next three weeks."

When it was time to report back for duty…

Well, he wasn't leaving her then, either. Since going AWOL wasn't a viable option, he had one choice: find out who was targeting her and put the creep behind bars.

# EIGHT

Shelby leaned against the diner's counter, staring at the cell phone in her hand. Her staff had left. The door was locked, the alarm set. But she had one more task to accomplish before heading upstairs.

She sighed. Conversations with her mother were never easy. Shelby's questions garnered one-word answers, and her mother never asked any of her own.

Until two and a half weeks ago, Shelby had phoned once a month. Now, she made that obligatory call weekly. With Mia gone, she was all her parents had left. They'd lost Lauren years ago.

She touched the phone icon next to the number she'd brought up a few minutes ago. She could have this conversation in the comfort of her apartment, but she'd rather be alone. Addy wouldn't understand. The woman hadn't provided details, but growing up on a farm in

Idaho, her childhood had to have been more pleasant than Shelby's.

Ryan was upstairs, too. All her arguments in the wee hours of yesterday morning hadn't swayed him in the slightest. He wasn't going anywhere.

After three rings, her father picked up. That was no surprise. Her mother rarely answered the phone.

Shelby chatted with him for several minutes, delaying the inevitable. The warm-up with her father was always the easiest part of the call. Though there'd never been warmth and laughter, their exchanges were at least two-way.

But something was different this time. There was hesitation, as if that aura of control he emitted was a facade that had finally sustained its first cracks. He was floundering, too.

A few minutes later, she heard rustling as he apparently rose from where he'd been sitting.

"I'll turn you over to your mother. Thank you, Shelby. She really needs these calls." Unspoken was a loud and clear "*I* need them."

"I'll stay in touch."

She'd filled him in on happenings at the diner, talked about Addy and even shared how Ryan was maintaining regular contact with his niece. But she hadn't mentioned the threats. Her parents didn't need the added burden of worrying about her and Chloe.

After some more rustling, her mother's "hello" came through the phone, flat and listless.

"I'm calling to see how you're doing." The false cheer she injected into her voice never had an effect on her mother, but she did it, anyway.

"I was napping."

Shelby didn't apologize. It likely wasn't the first nap she'd had that day.

She shared the same details she'd given her father, then asked about her mother's day. She'd made herself a ham-and-cheese sandwich for lunch, but hadn't made the bed. That was one way Shelby measured how well she was doing. If she got up and made the bed, it was a good day. There probably hadn't been any of those lately.

Finally, her mother released a sigh. It was heavy with sorrow, resignation and regret. "I'm going to let you go."

Shelby's own sigh escaped. At twenty-seven years old, she was still at a loss as to how to help her mother.

Maybe a visit would do what phone calls couldn't. Once the danger was over, she would leave the diner in Tessa's hands and spend a few days in Arizona.

"How about if I bring Chloe for a visit sometime? Would you like that?"

"Okay."

Shelby tamped down her disappointment at the lack of enthusiasm in the one-word answer. She'd never been able to make her mother happy. Why should now be any different?

When she was little, she would try hard to cheer her up. She'd take her mother's hand in her little ones and tighten her fingers. But her mother never squeezed back.

When she was in third grade, one of her friends said getting flowers always made her mother happy, so Shelby had picked a handful of wildflowers on her way home from the bus stop.

She'd found her mother staring out the window at the flower garden her father had planted for her. When Shelby passed her the bundle, her mother laid it on the table, then returned her gaze to the window, gift forgotten.

"When are you coming?"

The question pulled her thoughts back to the present. Was there a spark of hope underlying the usual monotone, an almost imperceptible lift in pitch?

"I can't get away right now. But soon. I promise."

She ended the call and headed upstairs, the image of those wildflowers lingering in her mind. She had followed her mother's gaze out the window, to the perfectly-shaped blooms covering the manicured bushes, the neatly mulched flower bed.

And she'd understood. Her scraggly gift couldn't hold a candle to what her father had done. Her wildflowers weren't ugly, just inferior.

But Shelby liked them, so she'd put them in water and kept them in her room until every bloom fell off and the leaves dried and curled. Those flowers were like her—nice by themselves, but inferior next to the others her father had produced.

When she opened the door at the top of the stairs, Ryan's smooth voice drifted to her. She stepped into the living room to find him sitting on the couch with Chloe in his lap, an open picture book in front of them. The little girl had already taken her nap. She'd been fast asleep when Shelby had come up around one.

Ignoring Addy's frown and arms-crossed pose, Shelby leaned against the wall to watch. Her father had never read to her. Neither had her mother. But Ryan wasn't like either of her parents. He was an amazing uncle. A perfect daddy.

As he finished the story, Addy crossed the room to slip past her down the hall. Ryan closed the book and looked over at Shelby with a smile.

He'd recently bought a bunch of picture books. Several were well-known Bible stories. In the one he'd just finished, Jesus had fed five thousand people with five loaves of bread and two fish.

Shelby walked into the room. As soon as she sat next to Ryan, Chloe reached for her, and she pulled the little girl onto her lap.

"Be-be." Chloe continued talking, even interjecting some hand motions. She seemed to know exactly what she was saying, though Shelby had no clue. But she was pretty sure she picked up "book" somewhere in the string of unintelligible words.

Shelby watched Ryan lean forward to place what he'd been reading on the coffee table. "Do you really believe that?"

He lifted a brow, his eyes shifting to hers. "Of course. Don't you?"

She shrugged. "I'm not sure." When she looked back at him, he was studying her. She frowned. "Don't look at me like that. You said you're not a religious person, either."

"I said I didn't attend church regularly. I still believe."

She leaned her head back against the couch. "When I was a child, my weekends with Aunt Bea always included church. Then I'd go home, and my dad would tell me that religion was a crutch for weak people. He likened those who believed in God to children refusing to let go of the myth of the Tooth Fairy."

"So you're agnostic?"

"No. I don't believe everything got here by chance. That's so scientifically improbable, it's easier to believe that a supreme being created it, or at least set everything in motion. I think God's out there somewhere. Maybe He notices what goes on down here, maybe He doesn't. But I think the Bible is just a book of stories written by men."

"What about your aunt?"

She pursed her lips. "She never missed a service and was involved in everything, from bringing food to shut-ins to leading a women's Bible study group to picking up people who could no longer drive and bringing them to church. But her religion didn't do her much good, because in spite of her prayers and the prayers of the church people, she died too young and suffered too much."

"Where do you think she is?"

"If there's a heaven, that's where she'd be."

"Then you can't say her religion didn't do her any good."

"I said '*if* there's a heaven.' That's a big *if*."

"Was she happy?"

Shelby met his eyes. "I never met anyone happier."

"Then her religion didn't hurt her. If she was wrong, she had nothing to lose, but if she was right, she had everything to gain."

Shelby rose from the couch. It had been too long a day for a philosophical discussion. "I'm going to make dinner."

After setting Chloe on the floor, she picked up the bin of toys and put it next to her. When she moved toward the kitchen, Ryan followed.

"Can I help with dinner?"

"Sure." He liked to stay busy, and she didn't mind accommodating him. Yesterday, he'd repaired the landing. Today, he'd popped down to the diner during Chloe's nap and bussed tables. She was going to miss him when he returned to duty.

Actually, it was more than that. His absence was going to leave a big void in both her and Chloe's lives. His time off had barely started, and she was already dreading when it would end.

Addy had told her not to fall in love with him. Shelby had tried to heed her advice. But it hadn't worked. Now she was dangerously close to doing exactly what Addy had warned her against.

The problem was, all her reasons for not getting romantically involved over the years didn't apply to Ryan. Instead of making demands, he gave more than he took. He never tore her down, only built her up. The one time he did judge her, he'd been man enough to apologize.

The attraction she felt toward him didn't help her cause, either. Seeing him dressed for duty each morning made her heart skip a beat. He always looked so strong and valiant. Irresistible. And that was in his camos and matching cap, pants legs tucked into his black boots. If she ever saw him in his service dress blues, she'd be done for.

She opened the refrigerator door and pulled out the package of hamburger she'd had thawing. A murmur of voices came from the living room. Addy had returned and was interacting with Chloe. With a loving aunt and uncle and doting nanny, the little girl never had to play alone for long.

Shelby closed the door and straightened. "I talked to my parents today. When this is over, I want to take Chloe for a visit."

"I'm sure they'll like that."

Addy's voice rose. "You're taking Chloe to Arizona?"

"Just for a visit."

She appeared in the doorway moments later. "I'll go with you."

Shelby's chest tightened just as it had when she'd tried to explain to her friends why her father was so gruff and her mother rarely left her room. Her family wasn't the same as other kids' families.

"That's okay. I won't need you since I won't be working." She softened the refusal with a smile. "It'll be an opportunity for some time off."

Addy's brows dipped toward her nose. "I don't mind. I'm happy to help take care of her so you can spend time with your family."

Shelby pulled a block of cheddar cheese from the fridge. Tonight she was making Aunt Bea's golden nugget burgers. She'd form hamburger patties around chunks of cheese, add some herbs and spices and pour a can of tomato sauce over the top. Quick and easy but tasty.

She laid the cheese on the counter next to the meat. "It'll just be a week. We'll be fine."

Both Ryan and Addy had met her parents at Mia's funeral. But a brief introduction at a funeral was a far cry from spending time in their home. The visit would be strained enough without her feeling the need to put up a front.

Eventually she'd have to make that leap with Ryan. There'd be family gatherings, holidays to celebrate. She knew how it would go. He'd be the unwanted visitor. Her mom would ignore him and her dad would find fault with him.

Addy lingered for several moments, her expression unreadable. When she walked away, Shelby turned her attention to making dinner. In a while, she'd give Ryan the job of peeling potatoes.

He leaned close and whispered, "She doesn't like to be told no."

Yeah, Mia hadn't, either. They'd probably made an interesting pair.

Shelby had decided to fire Addy if she had to. She hoped she wouldn't. Changing sitters would be one more upheaval in Chloe's life. Besides, Shelby felt sorry for Addy. The same way the little girl had filled a void in Dorothy McConnell's life, she was obviously filling a void in Addy's. She hadn't lost a child, but she'd experienced her own grief. When she'd had her hysterectomy, she'd lost the opportunity to birth a baby of her own.

Shelby pulled a plate from the cupboard, then tore into the plastic wrap covering the hamburger. At least she wouldn't have to think about holiday gatherings until Christmas. She and Ryan, and maybe Addy and Barry, would do Thanksgiving with Chloe at the apartment and figure out Christmas later.

As she began to separate the ground beef into seven comparable-sized chunks, she cast a glance at Ryan. She was worrying about nothing. Regardless of where they spent the holidays or how unpleasant the visit, Ryan wouldn't judge her family. It wasn't in his nature.

Besides, he hadn't grown up on the set of *Leave It to Beaver*, either.

In its own way, his childhood had probably been as messed up as hers had been.

An explosion ripped through the night, and bits of concrete rained down. Ryan dove behind the remains of what had moments earlier been the side of a building. Screams filled the air, along with the scent of scorched flesh.

He and five others had been on patrol when they'd spotted the young man in the distance, launcher resting on his shoulder. A second later, the rocket-propelled grenade came whistling in their direction.

Who was down? It was one of his men, but he wasn't sure who. He raised himself to a crouch and felt his way through the darkness. Where was everyone?

A volley of mortar fire brought down the rest of the building. Debris showered over him, trapping him beneath.

Ryan bolted upright, a scream working its

way up his throat. He clamped his mouth shut. There was no mortar fire. Afghanistan was half a world away. He was in North Bend. In Shelby's apartment.

He pressed a hand to his chest. His heart thudded and his T-shirt was damp with perspiration.

He'd dreamed he was back in Afghanistan. Four years ago, he'd served as an individual augmentee, a serviceman who deployed with a unit not his own. In his case, it had been a Marine detachment. The assignment had lasted twelve months. When he'd first returned to his regular duties, nightmares had plagued his sleep. Since then, they'd decreased in both frequency and intensity.

He drew in a breath, trying to calm his racing pulse, then froze.

There was no mortar fire, but something was burning. The odor was faint, barely detectable. The alarm downstairs began to squeal, and he sprang to his feet, thrusting aside the sheet. When he flipped on the light, the air was clear.

"Shelby!" He crossed the room in three large strides, then crashed into Addy who was exiting the hallway holding a still sleeping Chloe.

He grasped the woman's shoulders to steady her. "Something's on fire."

"I think it's the diner."

Just beyond her, the door to the interior stairs was open several inches. A gray haze wafted through.

Panic pounded up his spine. "Where's Shelby?"

"Probably still asleep. I'll wake her up. Get Chloe out of here." She pushed the child into his arms.

"Close that door." It would limit the smoke coming in and buy the women some time. Why was it even open?

"I will. Now go."

He spun and crossed the living room at a jog, swiping his keys and cell phone from the coffee table. Chloe was awake now and starting to wail. His panic was probably feeding hers. He'd soothe her later.

He grabbed his coat from the rack by the door and scooped up his tennis shoes and the clothes he'd worn yesterday. Before stepping outside, he glanced downward. No one had tampered with the stairs or landing.

When he ran around the side of the building, an eerie glow seeped from the edges of the miniblinds. With the windows covered, he couldn't tell how far the fire had progressed. Eventually, the second floor would cave in on the first.

He laid his clothes and shoes on the ground and looked back up the stairs, willing Addy and

Shelby to step through the still-open door. What was taking so long? *God, please get them out safely.*

The impromptu prayer brought him up short. The plea had sprung up without forethought. It was probably one he had no right to make. Yeah, he believed. But he wasn't in a place where he could expect any favors.

When Addy finally appeared with clothing draped over one arm, Ryan's knees almost buckled in relief. She'd even thought to grab Chloe's seal. But as she reached the bottom of the stairs, that relief disappeared.

"Where is Shelby?" He had to shout over the blaring alarm.

"Right behind me." Addy sounded winded. Her pulse was probably in overdrive, the same as his.

Several more seconds passed. What was Shelby doing, collecting personal items? Nothing was more important than her life.

"Take Chloe." If he had to, he'd drag Shelby out kicking and screaming.

Addy's eyes widened. "What are you doing?"

"Going in after her."

Addy looked as if she'd argue, then apparently decided against it. "Be careful. The floor was already warm. If you fall through, you're done." She dropped the items she held and reached for Chloe. "Tell her to leave her stuff and come on."

That was exactly what he intended to do. And throw her over his shoulder if she objected.

He took the stairs two at a time and burst through the open door. During the brief time he'd been outside, the smoke had grown much thicker. Where was it coming from? Had a portion of the floor caved in?

"Shelby, come on!"

No answer.

He pulled his T-shirt over his nose and hurried through the living room in a crouch. The fabric didn't make a good filter. His first breath induced a coughing spasm. His eyes watered and his lungs burned.

"Where are you?"

When he stepped into the hall, the door at the top of the diner stairs was still open, black smoke billowing through. Annoyance surged up inside him. He'd told Addy to close it.

He released a pent-up breath. Not everyone thought well under pressure. His military training helped. But he couldn't expect that of Addy.

He dashed down the hall toward the master bedroom. That had to be where she was. Annoyance surged up anew. She had a niece who depended on her, and she was gathering personal belongings while the apartment filled with smoke?

He barged through her open door, flipped on her light, then stopped short. She was still in bed, auburn hair flowing over her pillow, her body a long lump beneath the quilted comforter.

He slammed the door to keep out any more smoke, then stalked to the bed and shook her. "Shelby, wake up."

She stirred but didn't open her eyes. He threw open both windows to clear the air. What was going on? Addy had said Shelby was right behind her. Had she intentionally left her there to die?

No, that didn't make sense. If it was him lying there, maybe. But not Shelby. Addy liked her.

"Come on, Shelby." He shook her again. "The place is on fire. We've got to get out of here."

This time she spoke. Her tone held protest, but he couldn't make out the words. After throwing back the covers, he slid one arm under her knees and the other behind her back, ready to lift her.

She opened her eyes. It seemed to require some effort. "What's going on?"

"The diner's on fire."

She pushed herself to a seated position with a gasp that ended in a coughing fit. When she recovered, he swung her legs to the side and helped her to her feet.

"Grab some shoes and a change of clothes." Her coat was hanging the same place his had been. "We've got to get out of here."

He glanced around the room. Her phone sat on her nightstand next to an empty mug, the one she always used for her chamomile tea. Behind it was a framed photo of her and her aunt. He picked up the phone and slid it into the pocket of his shorts, then snatched the picture. Her purse was on the dresser, so he grabbed it, too. Hopefully her keys were inside.

Seconds later they were at the closed bedroom door, Shelby now fully alert.

"Take a deep breath and hold it until we get outside. The smoke's bad."

When they reached the bottom of the stairs, Addy was pacing the empty lot, arms wrapped tightly around Chloe.

She whirled on them. "What took so long?" She shouted over the squeal of the alarm and approaching sirens.

"Shelby was still asleep." He didn't try to hide the accusation or anger. If the woman wasn't holding Chloe, he'd probably wring her neck.

Addy's jaw dropped. "How? I woke her up. She told me to go, that she was grabbing a couple of things and would be right behind me."

"Then why was she still asleep when I got up there?"

"I don't know. I woke her up. I swear." Tears sprang to her eyes and clung to her lower lashes. "I thought she was right behind me. I did exactly what she told me—got my shoes and coat and came down."

Shelby started to cough, bending forward until she could breathe easily again.

"I'm so sorry." A tear slid down Addy's cheek. "I would never have left you if you hadn't told me to. You sat up and talked to me. I thought for sure you were awake."

Shelby put a hand on Addy's shoulder. "It's okay. I've always talked in my sleep. I've carried on entire conversations without waking up." She gave Addy a shaky smile. "It was a big source of entertainment for my older sister and her friends."

Relief flitted across Addy's face, and she gave Shelby a one-armed hug. "I'm so glad you're okay. When it took so long for you guys to come down, I was just about frantic. I'd have run up after you if I hadn't been holding Chloe." She gasped, her panicked gaze shifting to Ryan. "I think I forgot to close the hall door. I opened it, because I heard something. Then I smelled smoke and got Chloe. After running into you, I was focused on waking Shelby and getting out."

As he and Shelby struggled into their coats and tennis shoes, a fire truck pulled into the lot, and the fireman in the passenger seat jumped out. "Is anyone still inside?"

"No." He and Shelby answered simultaneously.

Shelby looked at the leather bag dangling from Ryan's arm. "You have my purse."

He handed it to her, and she fished out her keys. "This will save them kicking in the door."

While she unlocked it, he glanced at the firemen who had already unwound the hose and were preparing to enter. A broken doorjamb would have been the least of her worries.

As she walked back toward him, an explosion shook the building and she flinched. Since everything looked the same in the front, it was probably the kitchen.

She stopped in front of him, tears gathering on her lower lashes. "Aunt Bea loved this place. She put her whole life into it."

His heart twisted. He placed the frame he'd picked up facedown on the asphalt and stepped closer. Shelby might not appreciate an embrace, but she looked like she needed more than consoling words.

The moment he took her in his arms, hers came up to wrap his waist. She pulled him closer, her grip amazingly strong. He'd guessed right. She needed this hug.

And he did, too. He hadn't held a woman

like this since accepting the fact his wife's heart would never belong wholly to him. But having Shelby in his arms felt so right. Not just right, but what every fiber of his being longed for. He was like a starving man receiving nourishment for the first time in weeks.

A sob shook her shoulders. He pressed a kiss to her cheek and stroked her hair, the same way he often soothed his niece. "You can rebuild."

"I can bring the diner back." His heavy coat muffled her words. "But if the apartment is destroyed, there are things I'll never be able to replace. Keepsakes from Aunt Bea's life. Dozens of photo albums, so many memories."

"No one can take the memories away." He released her and picked up the frame. "But while you were getting your shoes, I grabbed this."

She took the picture and clutched it to her chest, tears welling anew. "Thank you."

A police car pulled into the parking lot, then an ambulance.

He tilted his head toward the ambulance. "Let them check you out."

"I'll be fine." She let out a cough again, trying unsuccessfully to stifle it.

He frowned. "You need to go. You inhaled a lot of smoke. I'll take care of Chloe. Once we know you're all right, I'll get you both somewhere safe."

The fire was probably unrelated to the other threats. The security alarm didn't sound until after it started, so it had to be accidental. Maybe an electrical short. If someone had broken in and started it intentionally, the alarm would have gone off as soon as the security system was breached.

His line of thinking was logical, but he couldn't shake the sense of dread that had settled over him. Someone had tried to kill Shelby and seriously injure him. Was it possible this same someone had found a way past the alarm and started the fire intentionally?

Ryan shook his head, everything within him rejecting the thought. The scenario was unthinkable, on two levels.

They'd had the system installed and been confident it would alert them of danger. If their assailant could slip past it while everyone slept, the alarm meant nothing. Just as unsettling was the extent of the man's cruelty.

What kind of person would burn down a structure with a sixteen-month-old child inside?

# NINE

Shelby put the plastic cover over the empty plate, then swung the table out of her way. Hospital food. It wasn't bad, but it wasn't her own cooking.

They'd taken her to Snoqualmie Valley Hospital and kept her for observation the rest of the night and all morning. Now she just wanted to go home. The doctor had promised it would be this afternoon, if she continued to do well.

Unfortunately, there was no more home to go to. At least not one that was habitable.

But the damage wasn't as bad as it could have been. The diner's kitchen was a total loss, and the rest of the restaurant had extensive damage. But other than some smoke, the apartment was untouched.

According to Addy, she'd already been awake, heard something and gone to investigate. Ryan had admitted to having a nightmare and waking up just before the alarm sounded.

Shelby had slept through everything, including Addy's attempt to wake her, as well as Ryan's first two attempts. She'd always been a heavy sleeper, but last night had been ridiculous. Maybe she needed to rethink her chamomile tea habit. It was supposed to relax her, not make her comatose.

But she wasn't complaining about how things had turned out. It could have been so much worse. Any of them could have died or been seriously hurt. Instead, they'd all gotten out. Over the past few hours, she'd thanked God several times. She wasn't even sure He'd had anything to do with it, but last night's conversation with Ryan had gotten her thinking. Maybe she shouldn't have listened to her dad all these years.

A child's voice drifted to her from down the hall. Moments later, Ryan stepped into the room holding Chloe, Addy trailing behind.

They'd all spent the night in the waiting room nearby, napping on chairs. Ryan had refused to go home, hovering until the nurse had run him out of her room. Although Addy had offered to take Chloe to Barry's and stay with her there, Ryan hadn't been willing to let the little girl out of his sight.

Shelby smiled at them. "How was lunch?"

She'd sent them out to eat when hospital staff had wheeled her own food in.

Ryan nodded. "It was good. We ate in the hospital cafe."

Chloe stretched out her arms. "Be-be."

Shelby lifted the sheet and patted the spot beside her. "You want to get in bed with Aunt Shelby?"

As Addy eased into the chair near the foot of the bed, Ryan lowered Chloe to the mattress. Right away, she reached for the control that adjusted the back of the bed.

Ryan sat in the chair he'd pulled up next to her in the early morning hours. "Any word about them sending you home?"

"Not yet." The motor beneath the bed hummed, and Chloe giggled as the back fully reclined. "The doctor promised me it would be this afternoon as long as I'm doing well. And I think I am." Her throat felt scratchy, and she still coughed occasionally, but she wasn't having any problems breathing.

"What then?" Addy asked.

The bed reversed direction until Shelby was again sitting up.

Ryan nodded. "I'm waiting for a call back, but I think I have that worked out."

The back of the bed started its downward movement again, and Shelby took the control.

"Okay, this is perfect. You're making Aunt Shelby seasick."

Chloe pointed to the red call button just out of her reach.

"Not that one. We don't want to bother the nurses." She grinned up at Ryan. "How do people handle twins?"

"That's a good question."

"So tell me about this place you think we can use."

Before he could respond, the ringtone sounded on his phone. He frowned at the screen. "I don't recognize the number."

During the conversation that followed, his responses didn't give anything away. But his expressions did. The caller didn't have good news. When Ryan finished, his mouth was set in a frown, and his eyes were stormy.

Shelby's chest tightened. "What's wrong?"

"That was the fire investigator. Everything's in the early stages, but there's evidence of possible arson. They wanted to warn us, considering everything that's happened."

The lunch Shelby had eaten seemed to congeal in her stomach. "How did they get in?"

"They don't know yet. One of the windows in the kitchen was broken. It appears to have blown outward, but they're still investigating."

Shelby swallowed hard, gaze fixed on the

thin, white blanket covering her legs. Something had snagged it. A thread was pulled partially through, its end resting in a lopsided S shape. It gave her something to focus on, to keep her mind from shattering into a thousand jagged pieces.

She'd been shot at and verbally threatened. Someone had tried to kidnap her niece, planted a bomb on her car and sabotaged her deck. This time they tried to destroy her home and her business.

She hoped Ryan planned to take her far away. Somewhere warm and sunny. Florida, maybe. Somewhere she could forget about the trauma she'd experienced and everything she'd lost in the past month.

Ryan put his hand over hers and squeezed. "We'll get through this."

He'd said that before. She lifted her gaze. When her eyes met his, understanding and compassion shot straight to her heart. How did he do that? How did he know what she was thinking without her saying a word?

Longing bombarded her, along with a desire to lean on him, to have him wrap his arms around her and be her strength.

From age twelve forward, she'd bolstered everyone else. Mia had needed and depended on her for everything. When Aunt Bea got sick,

Shelby had been the one to get her to doctors' appointments, take care of the household chores and keep the diner running. As Aunt Bea's condition deteriorated, Shelby had taken on increasingly more responsibility for her care.

She'd spent most of her life serving others. Now she was just tired.

Addy cleared her throat, the sound jarring in the silence. "Instead of making goo-goo eyes at each other, we need to come up with a game plan."

Heat crept up Shelby's cheeks, a combination of annoyance and embarrassment. Addy had warned her about Ryan. Even without the warnings, she wasn't under any delusions. If Addy couldn't spark his interest, Shelby didn't stand a chance.

"The only game plan right now is to get Shelby and Chloe away from North Bend." Ryan's voice was tight. He probably didn't appreciate Addy's comment, either.

When his phone rang again, he looked at the screen and smiled. "Our housing arrangements."

This call was even shorter than the other one. Less than a minute after answering, Ryan clipped the phone back at his side.

"It's set. My aunt has a vacation home near Snoqualmie Pass, up on the west summit. She keeps a key hidden outside. We'll leave the hospital, pick up a few supplies and head straight there."

Addy held up both hands. "Wait. Did you say your aunt?"

Shelby nodded. "My thoughts exactly. I don't want any member of your family knowing where we are."

"This is my mom's sister. She couldn't stand my dad when my mom was married to him. And my mom hasn't had contact with him since they divorced, other than times she had to when I was a kid. My aunt is the last person you'd have to worry about."

Shelby nodded, then frowned at Ryan. "Your father told me if I fought him for custody, I'd have every bit of the equity in the diner encumbered before I got to first base. He didn't tell me he planned to burn it down."

Ryan pursed his lips. "That move surprised me. My father doesn't care about you or Addy, and he certainly doesn't care about me. But I can't imagine him doing anything that would put Chloe in danger. Even though she's not Randall's child, he still wants to raise her badly enough to pay for the privilege. I think he figured with three adults in the apartment, someone would wake up and make sure she got out. But your diner would be destroyed."

Two soft raps sounded at the door, and Shelby

watched the doctor she'd seen that morning walk into the room. "How are you feeling?"

"Fine. Ready to get out of here."

He picked up the chart and skimmed the notes the nurse had made. "Any more coughing?"

"Not much."

"Shortness of breath?"

"None."

"Then I don't see any reason to keep you here."

She heaved a sigh of relief.

"Call my office if you have any problems." He made some notes, returned the clipboard to its place and walked from the room.

Addy rose and moved to stand next to Ryan. When Chloe lifted her arms, Addy took her then stood and rotated back and forth. "So you're headed to Ryan's aunt's place."

Ryan nodded. "Yeah."

"Are you sure it's safe?"

"Safer than staying in North Bend. No one will know where we are."

"Except your aunt." Suspicion laced her tone. Why did Addy always have to try to antagonize Ryan?

"Who is completely trustworthy."

"If you say so." She shrugged. "Can I go along to help with Chloe?"

Shelby shook her head. "It's probably not

necessary. I think two of us can manage one little girl."

She'd welcome any break she could get from the ever-present tension between Addy and Ryan. After witnessing it for almost three weeks, she placed ninety-nine percent of the blame with Addy. Maybe a hundred. Addy wasn't the first woman to be spurned. She needed to get over it.

Addy shrugged again. "I don't mind. But if you don't need me, I'll stay with Barry for the time being."

"Sounds good." Ryan's response was a little too eager.

Addy scowled at him. Shelby did, too. Yeah, one percent of the blame on Ryan.

An hour later, they were driving through the hospital parking lot in Ryan's Equinox, Chloe strapped into the car seat in the back. Addy had exited some time ago, sucking all the stress from the room when she left.

As Ryan turned onto Frontier Avenue, Shelby glanced in the side mirror. A Snoqualmie police cruiser pulled out behind them, something Ryan had arranged as soon as the hospital had completed her release paperwork.

He braked at the 99th Street stop sign. "We'll pick up necessities in North Bend."

Shelby nodded. The stop in North Bend

would involve a short jaunt off the interstate. Then they'd get back on and continue another twenty-five miles or so east, to get to the pass.

Ryan stepped on the gas and navigated the corner. One more turn put them headed toward the interstate. The hospital was a couple blocks off I-90.

"We'll hit Safeway for food. We also need to grab some clothes. Sweatsuits would be warm and comfortable. Any suggestions?"

"There's a Vanity Fair at the outlet mall."

"Good."

The light ahead turned red, and Ryan braked to a stop. On the left, a small green sign said Freeway Entrance.

Ryan glanced over at her. "I believe I saw an Ace Hardware, too."

"Yeah, over on Main. What do we need at Ace?"

"A snow shovel. The roads will be plowed, but I'd rather pull the Equinox into the garage."

Shelby watched the police vehicle follow them up the ramp. "What about them?" She tilted her head toward the mirror.

"They'll wait. I don't even have a toothbrush."

"That's the one thing I do have."

He lifted a brow. "You grabbed your toothbrush on the way out of a burning building?"

"No, you did. I keep a travel one in my purse, along with a sample-size tube of toothpaste."

"Always prepared."

"Sometimes." She stared out the windshield. Snow-capped mountains lined the horizon, the foothills of the Cascades. A gentle curve to the right brought Mount Si into view. "Tell me what your aunt's place is like."

"A-frame with a loft. Two bedrooms downstairs, one up. Rustic but really nice."

When Ryan pulled into a parking spot in front of Vanity Fair a few minutes later, the police vehicle continued down the row. It would either circle or find an advantageous place to wait. Although its presence was a relief, it was a vivid reminder that the danger was far from over.

Ryan snatched a cart that someone had left in front of the store. As he settled Chloe into the basket, his phone buzzed. He glanced at the screen and his jaw tightened. "Weather alert. There's a storm moving in, so we need to make this fast."

She nodded. He didn't have to explain. She'd lived in North Bend long enough to know that in bad weather, the Snoqualmie Pass area got dangerous quickly.

He wheeled the cart through the wood-and-glass door that Shelby held open. Moving past racks of clothing, they tossed items into the basket. Chloe sat swinging her feet and pointing, strings of nonsense words flowing from her mouth. If she was asking for anything, she wasn't upset about not getting it.

As they reached the front again, a police officer nodded at them from a short distance away. Good. An officer in the cruiser and one in the store. And Ryan at her side. It was the safest she'd felt in weeks.

When they walked from the store, the officer followed them out. The sky was the same steel-gray it had been when they left the hospital, but during the time they'd been shopping, a misty rain had started to fall.

While Shelby strapped Chloe into her car seat, Ryan tossed their purchases into the back, then returned the shopping cart. A quick stop at Ace garnered the snow shovel. After stocking up on food, they were back on I-90 headed toward the pass. The mist turned to rain, then flurries. By the time they exited onto Alpental, the wind had picked up, sending snow slashing against the windshield.

Shelby gripped the door handle, fear drawing her shoulders tight. Next to her, Ryan maintained a white-knuckled grip on the steering wheel. She flipped down the visor. Chloe sat framed in the mirror, clutching her seal and carrying on a one-sided conversation. She was the only relaxed one in the vehicle.

Ryan made a right onto Ober Strasse and began the final steep climb. Guye Peak was straight ahead, its snow-covered top scraping the sky. Snowbanks six feet high lined both sides of the road, edges cut vertical by the plow. If not for the A-frame minishelters protecting them, the fire hydrants would be inaccessible.

Ryan steered the vehicle between the walls of snow. Steep-roofed homes rose from a rolling blanket of white that extended in all directions. Driveways were empty, structures vacant. It was too early for the tourists looking to enjoy the mild summers.

Ryan stopped at the end of a driveway. The house stood before them, nestled against towering pines, its soaring front facade all glass. A porch wrapped three sides.

Shelby released the door grip one finger at a time, inhaling the air of tranquility that blanketed the scene. It was a place where people came to relax, to bond with and enjoy their loved ones.

She closed her eyes, trying to imagine something she'd never experienced as a child—a family that supported and encouraged one another, that appreciated each other and made time for fun. With Ryan beside her and Chloe in the back seat, the image seemed close enough to grab. A mother, father and child, embarking on a family vacation.

She opened her eyes and heaved a sigh. Her dream was nice, but there were two big problems.

Ryan had signed up for the father role in Chloe's life. He hadn't signed up for any role in hers.

And this was no vacation.

Not as long as someone was trying to kill her.

Ryan stepped from the bedroom Shelby shared with his niece and silently shut the door. Outside the large panes of glass, snow covered the deck and rose halfway up the lower windows, whipped against the house by hours of ferocious winds.

When they'd arrived yesterday afternoon, Shelby had gathered their meager belongings and taken Chloe inside while he'd shoveled the driveway enough to access the garage. Then they'd watched as the snow grew heavier and the winds increased, building to a mournful wail. Now they were snowed in. At least temporarily. Already, plows would be working to clear the pass, reaching the streets branching off I-90 before the day's end.

Ryan found Shelby in the kitchen, cleaning up

their lunch mess, which consisted of a couple of plates, knives and sandwich crumbs.

She cast him a smile over one shoulder. "Did she put up any fuss?"

"Not a bit. When I left the room, she was lying on her side, thumb in her mouth, staring at her seal."

Shelby rinsed a dish and put it on a towel she'd spread out on the granite countertop. "I'm glad Addy thought to grab it."

Ryan nodded. The Pack 'N Play his aunt kept on hand was a lifesaver, too.

He picked up a dish towel and dried what Shelby had washed. Although they'd bought some food items at Safeway, a small locked closet at the end of the counter contained canned and dry goods. His aunt had told him where she kept the key and said to help themselves.

Once they'd returned the dishes to their place in the cupboard, Ryan led Shelby back to the living room. A fireplace stood against one wall, built-in bookcases flanking either side. If it was up to him, he'd have already raided the stack of wood in the shed and had a roaring fire going. But announcing their position with smoke billowing into the sky wouldn't be wise.

The bank of exposed windows across the front made him uneasy enough. Once the plow finished clearing the snow, giving the outside world access again, he'd consider keeping the three of them closed up in the master bedroom. Although not as spacious and comfortable as the living room, it had a small sitting area with a couch and television.

He moved to the entertainment center that housed the big-screen TV. "How about a DVD while Chloe sleeps?" He grinned. "Something that isn't for kids."

She sat on the couch, returning his smile. "Life changes when you go from 'single' to 'single with child.'"

He agreed. But Shelby seemed to be adjusting well. Much better than he'd have anticipated earlier in the month. He opened one of the glass doors. "Romantic comedy? Sci-fi? Action-adventure?"

"I'm good with anything."

"We've got plenty of options. My aunt has been accumulating movies since she bought this place. It gives people something to do when the weather's bad."

He pulled a DVD from the shelf. "She does vacation rentals but keeps some weeks blocked out for friends and family. I knew she wouldn't mind us staying, but I had to make sure no one else had it booked."

"Are you guys close?"

"Not like you and your Aunt Bea were. We're

not estranged. I just haven't gotten to spend a lot of time with her."

He removed another DVD and added it to what he held. "My dad had primary custody so I spent a lot more time with him than my mom and her family."

"Usually it's the other way around."

He turned and leaned against the entertainment center. "My dad had the money for the better lawyers."

"Did your mom ever remarry?"

"Nope. I think ten years with my dad scared her off men permanently."

"Having met your dad, I can understand that."

He pulled a third DVD from the cabinet and approached Shelby. "How about one of these?"

He'd just handed her the small stack when his cell phone rang. Kyle Gordon's name was displayed on the screen. Ryan's pulse picked up speed. Maybe he had information about the case.

*Yeah, right.* Even if Kyle had information, he wasn't about to share it. They'd already been down that road.

But he couldn't keep the hope out of his greeting, anyway.

"You watching the news?" Kyle's gruff voice came through the phone, no-nonsense, all business.

"No, why?"

"Your dad's just been arrested."

The words slammed into him, knocking the breath from his lungs. Relief swept through him, guilt on its tail. Rejoicing over his dad's downfall seemed wrong.

"Turns out Mia Adair was right. There really was something going on at the club."

"What?"

"Your dad was involved in a human-trafficking ring—teenage girls. Some were runaways here in the US. Others were brought in from other countries. A few of them ended up working in his clubs."

"As dancers?"

"And more."

Ryan sank onto the couch, the ham-and-cheese sandwich he'd eaten churning in his gut. For most of his life, he'd placed too high of a value on women to be all right with his dad's activities. This was worse than he'd imagined.

Shelby looked over at him, eyebrows raised in question. He'd talk to her later. He had to finish absorbing the information himself before he could relay it to her.

Most of the women who worked in his dad's clubs were like Mia and Addy had been. They did what they did by choice. Maybe they didn't feel they had any other options. But they weren't held captive, forced to do things they didn't want to do. They finished their shifts and went home.

Kyle continued. "Mia had taken some pictures, kept them in some kind of cloud storage. We don't know what she was planning to do with them. Maybe blackmail your father."

Or try to secure a future with Randall. It wouldn't have worked. His brother was too selfish to sacrifice his own freedom for his father's, even if the prison he was avoiding was nothing more than marriage.

"So what's happening with his clubs?"

"The Seattle one is shut down permanently. The other locations are closed until investigations can be completed." Kyle heaved a sigh. "Sorry to lay all this on you, bro. But it looks like the stuff you and your friends have been going through might finally be over. With the evidence Adair captured, it's no wonder your dad had her killed to keep his activities secret."

When Ryan finished the call, he dropped his phone into his lap.

Shelby's eyes were still on him. "Good news or bad?"

He shook his head. "My dad's a bigger creep than I thought." He leaned forward, forearms resting on his knees, hands clasped between. "He's been involved in trafficking young girls."

Ryan didn't know any of them, hadn't seen

Mia's pictures. But that didn't stop the images from forming in his mind, based on ads he'd seen exposing the evils of trafficking. Teenage girls sitting on a concrete floor, arms and legs shackled. They all had the face of his little sister, Rachel. Or Chloe a decade or so from now.

The sandwich congealed and threatened to reappear. He swallowed hard. "Mia found out and took pictures. My dad had her killed to keep her quiet. And just in case, he tried to take you out, too." He closed his eyes. "My father has brought pain to so many people."

Somehow he'd find a way to restore a small portion of what his father had destroyed. If he ever got access to the old man's money, he'd see to it that each of those girls received something for the trauma they'd experienced. And Shelby…

She rested a hand on his back, then moved it in slow circles. "It's over. He won't be able to hurt anyone else." Her touch was comforting through the fabric of his sweatshirt. "What he's become has nothing to do with you. You couldn't have prevented any of this."

He straightened and turned toward her.

She let her hand fall to the couch between them. "Those girls will begin the healing process. I'll work on rebuilding the diner. And you can return to your life and not have to babysit me anymore." She smiled, but it didn't reach her eyes.

Was she telling him she didn't need him anymore? Wouldn't want him hanging around? A void opened up inside him. "As far as babysitting jobs go, I don't think I'm ready to give this one up."

Her smile faded, and her gaze locked with his. Her lips were parted, her chest rising and falling with shallow breaths. The air between them was heavy with emotion.

What was she feeling? Was she half as drawn to him as he was to her?

He leaned toward her. She narrowed the gap between them a little more. He dipped his head and moved closer.

She turned away, drawing in a shaky breath. "With your dad in prison, is there any chance your stepmom will try to take Chloe?"

Ryan sighed. He'd misread her signals. "My dad is the one who calls the shots. Without his influence, my stepmom won't have the means or incentive to pursue it further."

Shelby entwined her fingers, the small stack of DVDs beneath. "When she called, begging me to let her see Chloe, I could feel her sorrow through the phone. She's still grieving her daughter and granddaughter, and now she's lost Chloe."

Warmth filled his chest, mixed with a sense of longing that was almost painful. The more he'd learned about Shelby over the past few weeks, the more he'd come to admire her. No, not just admire. Love.

He could no longer deny it. He'd fallen in love with her. In spite of all the reasons he'd cited for remaining just friends, his heart hadn't listened.

Shelby skimmed the backs of the movies she held, apparently oblivious to the tug-of-war going on inside him. She handed him the third one. "I'm in the mood for action-adventure, now that my own is over." Her gaze shifted to the cold fireplace. "Does this mean we can build a fire?"

"Absolutely." He rose and slid the phone into his pocket. After retrieving the empty bucket sitting on the stone hearth, he headed toward the back door. A few minutes alone in the cold would give him an opportunity to clear his thoughts and rein in his emotions. "I'll be back in a few minutes with a bucket of wood."

When he stepped outside, the distant rumble of snowplows reached him. They were probably still on the interstate, working their way in his direction. He wasn't in a hurry. He could think of worse circumstances than being snowed in with Shelby.

As he walked toward the shed, a rolling blanket of white glistened in the sunlight, stretching all the way to the trees. Somewhere beneath was a mulched path. He knew it was there, because he and his mom had visited in the summertime.

He trudged through the snow, sinking to mid-calf. Without rubber boots, he was going to need the fire to dry out his tennis shoes and sweatpants. His socks were going to get soggy fast, too.

A padlock hung from the hasp holding the shed door shut. It was dummy locked, something else he remembered from prior visits. The firewood was available to anyone who knew where to look for it. When he stepped back into the house a few minutes later, his bucket held large and medium-size logs, as well as small bits to use for kindling.

Soon he had a roaring fire going. As the opening credits played, flames popped and sizzled nearby, filling the room with the scent of burning logs. It transported him back to those not-nearly-frequent-enough get-togethers with his mom's side of the family, as well as the few times he'd been able to escape with Kyle without his father finding out.

By the time the closing credits rolled on the screen, the fire had burned down to ash with a few smoldering embers.

"I'll bring in more wood, enough to last us

through the evening." Darkness was still several hours away, and Shelby seemed to be enjoying the fire, too.

When he stepped outside, the distant roar of a motor drifted to him. It was a different sound from the plows, which were closer now. Maybe someone was cutting up logs for firewood.

Inside the shed, he placed the metal bucket on the floor and arranged several logs. After depositing them in the flat, wrought-iron basket on the hearth, he stepped back outside. The roar was closer. Now it sounded more like a snowmobile engine than a chain saw. Apparently, someone was vacationing nearby after all.

He'd just finished filling the bucket a second time when his cell phone rang. This time it wasn't Kyle. The caller identified himself as Detective Harrington from Seattle PD, the lead on Mia's case.

"I'm calling to give you an update on the Mia Adair murder. I tried calling her sister, but it went to voice mail. I left a message."

He leaned against the opening to the shed. "I can relay what you tell me. I'm with her."

"I thought that might be the case." There seemed to be a smile behind the words. Everyone working the case knew about the threats and that he'd been staying at Shelby's to protect the women and Chloe. Kyle probably had everyone he worked with rooting for something to develop between him and Shelby.

Harrington's tone grew serious again. "Your dad's been arrested."

"I heard. It's on the news." He wouldn't risk getting his friend in trouble.

The detective relayed pretty much the same information that Kyle had given him.

"There's something else. It may not mean anything, but it's something you and Ms. Adair should know."

Uneasiness chipped away at the peace he'd felt for the past two hours.

"We checked out the background of everyone Mia Adair had been close to."

The snowmobile drew closer. "Including me?"

"Including you. Nothing raised any red flags. But something doesn't gel with Adelaide Sorenson."

*Addy.* "What?"

"One of the Snoqualmie officers made a comment in his report about Ms. Sorenson wanting to take the child to her parents' farm in Idaho, and the child's aunt refused."

"So?" That had happened several times.

"Ms. Sorenson's mother is a waitress at a diner in LA. She's never lived outside the city. And she was a single parent, didn't marry her child's father. Adelaide lived with her until she got an apartment at age eighteen. She moved to several locations in LA, until relocating to Seattle. Trudy Sorenson has never lived outside California, and until coming to Seattle five years ago, neither had Adelaide." He paused, as if for emphasis. "There is no farm in Idaho."

The snowmobile was even louder, moving toward one of the houses on the summit. The roar of its engine clashed with the alarms blaring in his head.

Why would Addy lie about something like that? Had she been planning to take Chloe and disappear? If so, why not just take her and run?

Because she was being watched too closely, confined within the four walls of the diner unless she stepped out alone.

The snowmobile was close now. In fact, it sounded like it was right in front of his aunt's house. The engine died and silence descended, heavy and ominous.

"I have to go." He pushed himself away from the doorjamb. "Someone just arrived on a snowmobile."

He was already at a full run when he slid the phone into his pocket and drew his weapon. As he reached for the doorknob, a familiar sound sent ice through his veins—the telltale click of the hammer being pulled back on a pistol.

"Drop it. Raise your hands."

Barry stepped around the side of the house, a SIG in his hand. "I said drop it."

Ryan stood frozen, confusion swirling through his mind. When he'd asked Barry if he had a gun, panic had flashed in his eyes. He'd said guns made him uneasy. Now he looked anything but. His hand was steady, his eyes cold.

Pieces of the puzzle began to fall into place. The shot fired at Shelby the night of Mia's murder, the man with the weapon on the streets of North Bend.

Guns didn't make Barry nervous. The flash of panic was because Barry was afraid Ryan suspected him.

More pieces fell into place. The man would do anything for Addy. Even the homemade bomb made sense, constructed by an admitted science geek.

"I'm not telling you again." Barry spat out each word. "Go ahead, give me an excuse to shoot you."

Ryan released his weapon. It landed silently, cradled in a thick blanket of white.

"Open the door and walk inside, hands up."

Ryan did as told, the despair settling over him, colder and heavier than anything last night's storm had dropped. He'd mentioned the snowmobile to Detective Harrington. But he hadn't asked the man to call for help.

When they'd been in North Bend, law enforcement had driven by regularly to check on them. That wasn't going to happen. Up here, no one would come.

He and Shelby were cut off from the rest of the world.

Completely alone.

# TEN

Shelby crouched behind the couch, peering over its back. A snowmobile had driven through the front yard and stopped right in front of the deck. It had held a single rider. That was all she'd seen before diving behind the sofa.

Maybe it was a neighbor coming to introduce himself, happy to not be the only one on the summit. Whoever it was, she'd let Ryan greet them. He was at least armed.

Except Ryan hadn't come in from getting firewood. The first trip had taken less than two minutes. Now he'd been out there at least five. What if something had happened?

She needed to get to her phone, but it was in her purse, which she'd left in the bedroom where Chloe was sleeping. She crept toward the closed door ten feet away. There was nothing to hide behind, no shadows to conceal her movement. With the sun shining through the soaring wall of windows, there wasn't a dark spot in the room.

When she looked in that direction, the rider had gotten off the snowmobile. Large sunglasses hid the upper part of his face. Even in the bulky parka, the person didn't look very large. Shelby squinted into the sunlight. Maybe she was looking at a woman.

The rider removed the helmet, and jet-black hair tumbled over her shoulders. Shelby heaved a relieved sigh. She never thought she'd be so happy to see Addy.

As she swung the front door inward, the back one creaked open. She gave Addy a welcoming smile. "I guess you heard the good news." She'd probably watched the same report Ryan's friend had mentioned and come to celebrate. The snowmobile likely belonged to Barry.

Addy's eyes shifted beyond Shelby, and her features darkened. She'd seen Ryan, but this time, it was more than annoyance, or even dislike. There was a hardness in her eyes Shelby had never seen before—hatred, cold and lethal.

Shelby turned, a sense of dread she couldn't explain showering down on her. Ryan was walking toward them, arms lifted, Barry behind him.

Dread turned to confusion, then denial as Barry stepped to the side. He held a weapon.

Barry didn't own a gun. He'd said so. He hated guns. But here he was, pointing one at Ryan.

Barry had lied.

Shelby spun on Addy. "What's going—"

Her gaze locked on the barrel of a pistol. The rest of the words froze in her throat.

Addy aimed the weapon at her chest. "Where's Chloe?"

"Taking a nap in the bedroom." Where she'd left her phone. "I'll get her." If she could manage a whispered 911 call, they might stand a chance.

"I'll go with you. I don't want you trying anything."

Shelby's heart fell. When she walked into the room, Addy followed. Chloe was just starting to stir.

Shelby bent over the playpen and patted her back. "Hey, sweetie. It's time to get up. Addy's here."

Chloe sat up and pulled herself to her feet. "Addy." She stretched out her arms then drew them back. The little girl didn't know enough to be afraid of guns, but instinctively knew something was wrong. When Shelby lifted her from the bed, Chloe twisted to look at Addy and started to cry.

"Shh, sweetie. It's okay." Shelby jiggled her, but the more she tried to soothe her, the harder she cried.

Addy stared at them, lips curled in a sneer. "Can't you do anything right?"

Shelby flinched. The words were like daggers, piercing places that had scabbed over years ago, and she was once again that little girl trying unsuccessfully to please her father. How many times had she heard those exact words, uttered with the same disdain?

Addy continued. "No one should have ever given Chloe to you. That cop at Mia's place was an idiot."

Shelby squared her shoulders. She wasn't an insecure little girl. She was a responsible, confident adult. If she had any chance of talking her way out of the situation, she was going to have to pull together her scattered thoughts.

"What do you want?"

"All I've ever wanted. Chloe."

"You have her. You've always had her." She shook her head. None of this made sense.

Shelby motioned toward the gun. "This is unnecessary. Robert McConnell is in jail. The danger's over. Ryan will go back to his apartment, and it'll just be you and me and Chloe. You'll be with her all the time, just like before Mia was killed."

A block of ice slid down Shelby's throat and settled in her gut. Maybe it wasn't Ryan's father who'd had Mia killed.

Everything had pointed to him. Mia had said she'd uncovered something at the club, something that could get her killed. The authorities had even found proof in her pictures.

But maybe he didn't know what Mia had found and Addy had simply seized an opportunity. She'd struck, then led the authorities down the wrong path, knowing all along she'd be the least likely suspect.

But why kill Mia when she already had what she wanted?

Addy tilted her head toward the door. "Take her out to the living room."

Shelby stepped from the room with a screaming Chloe. Ryan sat on the couch, and Barry stood with his back against one of the bookshelves flanking the fireplace. His weapon was trained on Ryan, his hand steady, his posture poised. Where was the nervous, insecure man who regularly visited Addy?

He was standing right there, the same person he'd always been. Except now, he was doing what Addy wanted, with no risk of incurring her anger. How far would he be willing to go in his desire to please her?

Addy gave Shelby a nudge with the barrel of the pistol. "Sit next to Ryan."

"Addy." Ryan's voice was soothing, but his tone held an underlying tightness. "Please don't do this. You love Chloe. Think of what's best for her."

"Shut up!" The command came from Barry. "You open your mouth again, that'll be just the excuse I need to shoot you."

Shelby raised a hand. "It's okay. Everybody needs to stay calm." If Addy would slash her best friend's throat to take her child, she wouldn't hesitate to kill Shelby and Ryan.

As Shelby approached the couch, she met Ryan's gaze. Did he have a plan? He had to. He was trained to get out of dangerous situations. Through twenty years in the military, he'd probably escaped worse than this.

The odds were even—two against two. Ryan was a lot bigger than Barry. But Barry was armed. Ryan was, too. But the way Barry was watching him, he'd never be able to draw his weapon and fire without taking a bullet himself.

Unless she could get to it without Barry noticing, then distract him long enough to put it in Ryan's hand. Ryan sat in the center of the couch. He was right-handed. That was the side where she'd find his weapon.

She rounded the coffee table and eased down beside him, positioning Chloe on her left leg. When she pressed the back of her forearm against Ryan's side, her heart fell. The holster was empty.

Ryan was unarmed. And if he so much as opened his mouth, Barry would shoot him.

That meant everything rested on her.

"Where is Chloe's stuff?" Addy's question sounded more like a command.

"Everything's in the dresser in her room."

Addy nodded toward Barry. "Keep an eye on them. If either of them tries anything, shoot them."

Shelby watched her disappear into the bedroom. Addy's mind was made up. She wanted Chloe, and nothing was going to stop her. She'd been so sure her position as godmother would give her what she needed to get custody. It hadn't worked. So she'd tried repeatedly to convince Shelby and Ryan to allow her to leave with Chloe. That hadn't worked, either.

Now Addy planned to do the unthinkable—kill her and Ryan and kidnap Chloe. There was no way she would keep them alive. Otherwise, she and Barry wouldn't make it out of the county before the authorities stopped them.

Addy tramped from the room, a pile of clothing and diapers in her arms. "What about food?"

"There's a six-pack of applesauce and Goldfish crackers in the pantry, bananas on the counter, string cheese in the fridge. Take whatever else you want."

As Addy disappeared into the kitchen, a low rumble seemed to come from somewhere in the distance. A snowplow was on the summit, possibly moving in their direction. Not that it was going to do them any good.

When Addy returned a few minutes later, she held two plastic bags. She'd stuffed Chloe's clothing into one and filled the other with food. The pistol's barrel was tucked into the waistband of her jeans.

"I'm securing all this on the back of the snowmobile. Then we'll be ready to go."

Addy stepped out the front door, pulling it shut behind her. Within minutes, she'd walk back in, and it would be all over.

Shelby sat up straighter. Addy's mind was made up, but maybe she could appeal to Barry.

"I know you love Addy, but do you really want to be involved in this? You're a good man. And you're smart—smarter than any of us." Unfortunately, when Addy was around, Barry seemed to lose the ability to make rational decisions.

"Think what this will mean." She talked fast. Addy had already reached the snowmobile. She wouldn't be out there for long. "You three will spend the rest of your lives on the run. That's assuming you don't get caught, which isn't likely."

His jaw tightened, but his eyes were unreadable.

"You don't want to hurt me. Ryan, either. I don't know what Addy has told you, but he's never done anything to you."

Barry spoke through clenched teeth. "He keeps trying to take Addy from me."

Ryan tensed, and she willed him to stay quiet. Outside, Addy straightened and turned from the snowmobile.

"That's not true. Addy's manipulating you." Shelby took Ryan's hand and entwined her fingers with his. "Ryan's not interested in Addy. He and I are a couple now."

Hopefully, God would forgive her for the lie. Considering she was trying to save his life, Ryan should, too.

He squeezed her hand. He was only playing along, but his grip was reassuring.

Doubt flashed in Barry's eyes, and his reserve seemed to falter. Addy lumbered closer, leaving deep footprints in the snow. Perspiration coated Shelby's palms.

"Addy's a user. As soon as she's finished with you, she'll throw you away. You've seen how she treats you, hot one minute, cold the next."

Addy was climbing the steps now. Shelby's pulse jumped to double time. If there was anything else that might sway Barry, she had only seconds to say it.

"You're a great guy, Barry. You're kind, devoted. You deserve better."

The front door swung open and Addy stepped inside. After closing the door, she lowered herself to one knee and held out her hands. "Come here, sweetie pie."

Chloe buried her face in Shelby's shirt.

"Put her down." Ice laced Addy's tone.

Shelby tried to lower Chloe to the floor, but the little girl curled into a ball, clinging to Shelby's clothes.

"It's okay, sweetie. You have to go with Addy."

"Noo-o-o-o!" The word was a wail.

Addy rose and stepped forward, casting Barry a glance over one shoulder. "If either of them tries anything, shoot the other one."

With one knee on the coffee table, she bent forward and snatched up the little girl. Shelby gasped. It was the first time she'd seen Addy be rough with Chloe.

Chloe screamed more loudly and reached for Shelby. Addy gave her a rough shake. "Chloe, stop it."

Shelby held up her hands. "Addy, please. You won't get away with this. Your parents' farm is the first place the authorities will check."

Addy laughed, harsh and mocking. "I never knew my father, and my mother doesn't have a farm in Idaho."

Shelby's jaw dropped. Another lie. With Addy, everything was a lie.

"Don't look at me like that. This is your fault." She rotated from side to side, trying to calm Chloe. She wasn't any more successful than Shelby had been. "If you'd stayed in North Bend, we wouldn't be here."

Barry shifted his weight from one foot to the other. That calm demeanor was showing some cracks. He didn't deal well with crying children. "Come on, Addy. Let's get out of here."

Addy ignored him, eyes still on Shelby. "It was supposed to be so simple. I'm Chloe's god-mother. With Mia out of the way and Randall in jail, she was supposed to be mine. Instead, you showed up."

"Why kill Mia? You had everything you wanted."

"Mia was taking Chloe away."

"But you could have gone with her."

"No, I couldn't. Mia said she didn't need me anymore, said that I was getting too posses-sive of Chloe." Her voice was raised to project over Chloe's screams, the volume amplifying the hurt and anger she apparently still felt. "It wasn't fair. I wanted a child so bad, but for Mia, Chloe was just a way to try to get to Randall. She didn't deserve her. I do."

"So you had Barry slit her throat while she napped."

Barry shook his head violently, eyes wide. "That wasn't me."

"I did it." In spite of the volume, Addy's tone

was nonchalant. "When I got back from Safeway, she was still asleep. I put Chloe in her room then took care of Mia. Then I called the police, saying I'd found her like that when I walked in."

Shelby's heart clenched. Killed in her sleep by her best friend, someone she trusted wholeheartedly. "Did she know?"

"Know what?"

"That it was you."

"Yeah. It took time for her to bleed out enough to lose consciousness."

Shelby slumped, bile churning in her stomach. When she shifted her gaze to Barry, her own horror was reflected on his face. Either hearing the details bothered him, or like everyone else, he'd believed that Ryan's father had ordered Mia killed.

Shelby shook her head, trying to clear the confusion. If Addy killed Mia, what about all the threats? "Who shot at me in Mia's parking lot?"

"Barry."

"I didn't try to hit you." He spoke fast, his tone defensive. "Addy called me, told me to fire a shot to scare you. I waited at the end of the road for her to text me when it was time."

While Shelby had stood with Ryan outside Mia's apartment door, Addy had gone downstairs. She'd been gone only a few minutes, but it had been plenty of time to make that phone call.

Addy shifted Chloe to her other hip and held her close. The little girl was finally calming down. Maybe she'd worn herself out.

Addy continued. "I figured if you thought Chloe was in danger, you'd let us take her."

Ryan's father had tried to take her, too. That couldn't have been set up by Addy. He'd spoken with Shelby himself and made his threats.

"Who barged into the apartment and tried to take Chloe?"

"Nobody. That was a setup."

Once again, she'd taken advantage of an opportunity. After Robert McConnell's failed attempt to get Chloe, Shelby had automatically suspected him.

"But someone hit you." There was no way she could have done that herself.

"Barry."

"I didn't want to do it." Regret filled his tone.

"I made him hit me. It almost killed him."

"You orchestrated everything." Shelby shook her head. "Ryan's father was never a threat."

Addy nodded. "Barry was the mysterious man with the gun."

Shelby looked at Barry, brows raised. "You're the one who attacked Ryan?"

"He didn't give me a choice. He was gaining on me. I hid behind a bush, then jumped out and hit him with the side of my gun. If I'd wanted to kill him, I would have shot him."

Addy picked up where she'd left off. "Barry slashed Ryan's tires, then scraped up the door and jamb to make it look like someone had tried to break in. He made the bomb and planted it on your car."

Barry cut in again. "It wouldn't have exploded. I intentionally didn't get the mix right."

Addy ignored the interruption. "As far as tampering with the deck, we were both happy to try to get rid of him." She tilted her head toward Ryan, mouth set in a scowl.

Shelby tried to blink away her confusion. Things weren't adding up. "But the masked person in the video was stockier than either of you." They'd checked the feed numerous times.

Addy nodded. "Several layers of clothes a couple sizes too big can be pretty convincing. Your location made it simple—an alley that's often deserted, bordered by trees. Barry would park a few spaces down, out of view of the camera and approach through the woods. When he finished, he'd shed the extra clothes and mask, move the car down and arrive like normal." She frowned. "But you were too stubborn to heed the warnings. So I had to step up my game."

"The fire."

A twisted smile curled her lips. "That was all me. I slipped downstairs with some newspaper and a coffee can of gasoline I'd had Barry bring over."

That was why the alarm hadn't gone off until after the fire had started, why the only broken window appeared to have been blown outward.

Realization slammed into her with the force of a freight train. She'd made her tea, then left it steeping on the counter while Ryan had read Chloe a bedtime story. She'd thought she was sleeping exceptionally heavy. Now she knew the truth.

"You put something in my tea, hoping I wouldn't wake up."

"Two of my sleeping pills. It would have worked if he hadn't insisted on running back up after you."

"But why do all this now?" Addy's possessiveness had disturbed Shelby enough to think about letting Addy go once the danger was over, but she'd kept those thoughts to herself.

"You were planning to take her away, like Mia was."

"No, I wasn't."

"You were taking her to Arizona."

"I was coming back."

"That's what you said. But what if you stayed

and I never saw Chloe again? I couldn't take that chance."

Addy moved to the front door. When she swung it open, the faint rumble Shelby had heard filled the late afternoon air. The plows were closer than she realized, maybe even on Ober Strasse. With their four-wheel-drive SUVs and the help of the plows, police would be able to reach them. But no one knew she and Ryan were in trouble.

*God, please help us.* The silent plea felt awkward. She'd thanked Him for saving them from the fire. But throwing a prayer of thanks out there, just in case, was a lot different from asking for something and having faith to believe He cared enough to answer, or even heard.

Addy stepped into the opening, and Barry started to follow. She glared at him. "You're not finished."

He furrowed his brow. "What do you mean?"

"As soon as we leave, they'll call the cops."

"We can take their phones."

"They can identify us, you idiot. As it stands, no one suspects us."

Shelby's words tumbled out, her tone frantic. "The authorities don't suspect you now, but when you disappear, you'll both be suspects."

"Not if we ransack Barry's place and make it look like we were both abducted."

"You'll spend your whole life running. You don't want that for yourselves or Chloe."

"Don't tell me what I do or don't want." She leveled her gaze on Barry. "Shoot them."

Barry held up one hand. "Whoa, wait a minute. I agreed to try to scare them into letting us take Chloe, because that's what you wanted. I was even okay with sabotaging the landing so Ryan would fall through, because you told me he was trying to take you away from me." He tucked the barrel of the gun into the back of his pants. "I draw the line at murder. If you want to kill them, you're on your own. I'm leaving."

He'd taken one step when Addy slammed the door. Chloe flinched and started to scream again. After shifting the terrified child to her left hip, Addy drew her weapon. "You're not going anywhere."

"Come on, Addy." He raised both hands and stepped backward. "I love you." He took another step. "I've done everything you've asked."

Addy's eyes narrowed. "I won't let you bail on me now."

Barry continued his slow backward steps. He'd almost reached the kitchen. "I'm not a killer."

"If you won't do this for me, you're not worthy of my love."

"And if you ask me to do this, you're not worthy of mine."

Addy's jaw tightened, and coldness entered her eyes. Barry read the silent signal. He spun and ran for the back door at the same time a blast reverberated through the house. As he dropped to his knees at the end of the kitchen cabinets, Chloe released an ear-piercing scream that went on and on.

Addy gave her a shake. "Chloe, hush."

Chloe fell silent long enough to draw in a breath for another scream. Addy aimed the pistol at Ryan. Shelby's heart stopped, then resumed an erratic rhythm, slamming against her rib cage. She needed to say something, but her mouth had gone dry, and her brain had stalled out.

When Ryan held up both hands, Shelby's panic ratcheted up several notches. *Don't talk.*

He ignored her silent plea. "You won't make it out of King County." He shouted the words over Chloe's wails. "You're already a suspect. I talked to the detective. They know you lied about the farm."

"I don't believe you."

"Your mother is a waitress in LA, has lived there all her life."

Addy's eyes widened and her jaw went slack.

She recovered immediately. "By the time anyone discovers your bodies, I'll be several states away."

"They'll stop you before you get off the summit. I was on the phone with the detective when you arrived. They know you're here."

Chloe's cries grew less hysterical, allowing Ryan to lower his voice. "If you kill us, Chloe will go into foster care. Think how traumatic it will be for her, losing everyone she knows. You don't want that."

Addy's eyebrows drew together, parallel creases forming between them. Ryan's arguments were getting to her.

He continued his calm assault. "You love Chloe. Everything you've done is because of your love for her. The courts will take that into consideration."

Addy set her jaw, cold determination filling her eyes. "If I'm going down, you are, too."

Chloe stopped crying to take several hiccupping breaths. In the relative silence, the rumble of the snowplow was more obvious. But there was something else, too—the higher pitch of a vehicle's engine.

Addy spun toward the front windows with a gasp. Ryan sprang to his feet, leaped over the coffee table and slammed into her.

As the three bodies crashed to the floor, Addy's furious roar blended with a renewed scream from Chloe. A second ear-splitting crack filled the room, and a lamp next to Shelby shattered.

Chloe scrambled away from the struggling adults, then curled up on the floor, sobs wracking her little body. Ryan wrestled the weapon from Addy and slid it across the polished wood floor. It came to a stop under the coffee table.

Shelby left it there. She was already on her feet, stumbling toward Chloe, arms extended. Prayers of thanks circled through her mind. Ryan was alive, and so was she. As she reached her niece, the front door burst open, and a uniformed police officer stepped inside, drawn weapon sweeping the room. Behind her, someone entered from the back.

She lifted Chloe from the floor, hoping she was only frightened. Ryan had taken a chance tackling Addy with Chloe in her arms. But if he hadn't, he and Shelby would be dead.

Now he had Addy pinned facedown, hands behind her back, while she shouted curses at him. The officer stepped farther into the room. "Is everything secure?"

Ryan swiveled his head. "Yes. The woman here is the only threat. But the man down in the kitchen needs medical help stat."

Shelby sank onto the love seat and cast a

glance in that direction. Barry was still alive. Although she hadn't been willing to take her eyes off Addy while she'd held the gun on them, regular moans had come from the kitchen. Even now, he writhed in pain, his legs bending and straightening. The other officer knelt next to him, talking softly into his radio. Shelby wrapped her arms around the sobbing child in her lap and held her close.

As soon as the officer had cuffed Addy, Ryan rose. When he reached the love seat, he shook his head, his eyes moist. "I almost lost her. And I almost lost you."

He dropped to his knees and wrapped both of them in his arms, the side of his face pressed against Chloe's back.

Shelby closed her eyes. The warmth of his presence wrapped around her, providing a sense of security she hadn't felt since…ever. She couldn't explain it. Her diner was ruined and her savings wiped out. She was responsible for the fragile little girl in her lap and had no idea what challenges she'd face in the coming weeks.

But with Ryan at her side, she'd make it through. Even if his involvement was only as a friend to her and a father figure to Chloe.

He rose and sat next to her, one arm draped across her shoulders, the other hand holding Chloe's. Through the interviews by the police officers and the arrival of the paramedics, he remained like that, holding her in a one-armed hug. She didn't make it something it wasn't, even when he pulled her tightly against this side. Emotions were high. Once they both calmed down, they would transition back to the friendship they'd shared.

When the police officer walked away, Ryan leaned close, his warm breath brushing her ear. "Do you still doubt the existence of a personal God who cares for His creation?"

She turned her head to look at him. She had prayed, with no confidence that God would hear. But God had answered, anyway. He'd actually begun to orchestrate events before she'd sent her brief panicked prayer skyward.

The call from the detective had come at exactly the right time. Ten minutes earlier, the conversation would have been over before Addy and Barry arrived. Ten minutes later, and Ryan wouldn't have been able to answer his phone.

She smiled up at Ryan. "Actually, I've been talking to Him, and I've come to the conclusion that my dad was wrong about a lot of things."

She shifted her gaze to the kitchen, where the paramedics were working to stabilize Barry. According to one of the officers, a medevac chopper was on its way to airlift him to the nearest trauma center. Shelby prayed he'd hang on. How could such a bright young man allow himself to be manipulated so badly?

Some time later, after police had left with Addy and Barry was on his way to the hospital, Ryan stoked the fire and added more wood. Chloe was sound asleep in the bedroom, exhausted from their earlier ordeal.

Ryan straightened. For several moments, he stood facing the fire. When he finally turned, his gaze was warm. "You told Barry we're a couple now."

Heat crept up her cheeks. "I'm sorry. I was just— That was to convince Barry that you're not his enemy."

A while ago, he'd acted like he wanted to kiss her. It was what she'd wanted, too, and she'd almost let him. But she couldn't allow them to cross that line. Once they did, she'd fall hard. When it didn't work out, their interactions would be awkward and uncomfortable.

Ryan moved toward her without speaking. Was he mad at her? Did he think she was trying to push him into a relationship, like Addy had tried to do?

He had nothing to fear. She was too practical to harbor unrealistic expectations. Not long ago, she'd asked him what kind of woman was his type. She'd stupidly hoped it might be her.

He'd said, "No one." He wasn't interested in a relationship, period.

She rushed to explain. "That was for Barry's benefit. Trust me, I'm perfectly content to just be friends."

He sat next to her and once again draped an arm over her shoulder. His nearness was making her jittery. Before, there'd been an excuse. They were both reeling from almost losing their lives. And they'd had an upset child to comfort.

Now, that child was asleep, some time had passed and their emotions had returned to normal.

So why was Ryan looking at her like that?

"What if I'm not content with just friendship?" His voice was soft, filled with tenderness.

Her throat constricted in an odd mix of anxiety and anticipation. This was exactly how her parents' relationship had started, how almost every long-term relationship began. That decision to move from friendship to something more. It was a small step, but held huge potential. For happiness or disaster.

She wasn't ready.

"I—I don't know." She dropped her gaze to her lap.

He laid his free hand over both of hers, which she had clasped in a white-knuckled grip.

"Shelby, we're not making a lifetime commitment. I'm asking for a few dates, an opportunity to get to know each other without threats hanging over us. I'd like to give it a try and see where it leads."

What he'd said was tempting. She'd been fighting her attraction to him almost from day one. As she'd spent more time with him, attraction had grown into respect and admiration. Watching him with Chloe had chipped away at her resolve even further.

He'd said he wanted to see where it led. But what if it led the same place as her parents' relationship? What if she eventually found herself in the same prison her mother had inhabited for the past thirty-five years?

Ryan squeezed her hands. "What are you afraid of?"

What was she afraid of? Everything. She was afraid that Ryan would go into this with unrealistic expectations, then realize that he'd gotten an inferior product. She was afraid that she'd fall head over heels for him, and someone prettier or smarter or more talented or more fun would come along and steal his heart. And she was afraid of losing herself, afraid that as Ryan shaped her into who and what he thought she should be, the strong and independent woman she was now would disappear into the mist.

Ryan released her hand. "You know I was married before. You might have even guessed my wife was unfaithful. What you don't know is that you two were born within a few weeks of each other. And she's beautiful, just like you."

Warmth spread through Shelby's chest at the compliment, even while her mind protested. She wasn't the pretty one—Mia was.

He heaved a sigh. "But she was restless. At first, I blamed the age difference. Then I blamed myself, that I didn't have what it took to hold on to her."

He hooked an index finger under her chin and gently lifted, encouraging her to meet his eyes. "The idea of trying a serious relationship again scares me to death. But these past weeks together, I've fallen in love with you. I can't walk away from this without at least seeing if we can make it work."

He lowered his arm from her shoulders and took her hand, entwining her fingers in his. "Neither of us grew up in the best home. And we've had bad experiences since. We've both got baggage that makes us want to run in the opposite direction." He squeezed her hand. "I think it's time to let go of those fears instead of allowing them to shape our futures. Think about it, Shelby. I'm not asking you to do anything I'm not willing to do myself."

His gaze held hers, his eyes heavy with a silent plea. How could she deny him when he looked at her like that? If he was willing to risk his heart, couldn't she find the courage to risk hers?

"I've been fighting feelings for you almost from the start." She gave him a shaky smile. "It hasn't worked. As hard as I've tried not to, I've fallen in love with you, too. But it'll be a while before I'm ready to jump into anything. You'll have to be patient."

His lips lifted in a hopeful smile. "I'm willing to go as slow as you want to go. Turtle speed. Even snail speed."

"Glacier speed?"

"As long as we're moving forward, I'll be happy."

He squeezed her hand, and she squeezed his back. When he dipped his head and leaned toward her, her heart fluttered. He was going to kiss her. She wasn't sure she was ready for that, either.

The first brush of his lips quelled her fears. His kiss was gentle, demanding nothing, giving rather than taking. As she released the final shred of resistance, all the tension drained from her body, replaced by warmth and contentment.

She'd made her decision. She was dropping her guard completely, putting her heart in Ryan's hands. She should feel as if she was dangling over a precipice.

But she didn't.

If she was, it wasn't nearly as scary as she'd envisioned.

Because something told her she could trust Ryan to be her safety net.

# EPILOGUE

"Twain!" Chloe jumped up and down, one hand wrapped in Ryan's, the other in Shelby's. Ryan looked at her, her excitement bringing a smile.

The three of them had just walked out of the Northwest Railway Museum, where Chloe had been fascinated with all the colorful old railroad cars. Now they were getting ready to board for the next stop on their North Bend/Snoqualmie train excursion.

Three months had passed since Addy's arrest. Barry had survived and was cooperating with the authorities. Addy probably wouldn't see freedom until she was an old lady, if even then.

Chloe acted like a typical one-and-a-half-year-old. Her resilience still amazed him. Five days a week, she went to day care and loved it. The first time Shelby had dropped her off at The Little Ark, Chloe had cried and clung to her. A few hours later, she hadn't wanted to go home.

As far as a relationship with God, Ryan's "someday" had finally come. Every Sunday found him with Shelby and Chloe at her aunt Bea's church. Shelby's only regret was that Aunt Bea hadn't lived long enough to see her favorite niece experience the love of a Heavenly Father.

As soon as they boarded the hundred-year-old train, Ryan let Chloe lead them down the aisles to the last car. It wasn't as luxurious as the passenger coach they'd chosen for the first part of the excursion, with its wooden interior and plush red seats. The large side doors were open, a board fastened halfway up with wire mesh beneath for safety. Instead of bench seats, wicker chairs were arranged haphazardly around the space.

Chloe pushed him toward one. "Sit."

As soon as he removed his backpack and settled in a chair, Chloe climbed onto his lap. Shelby sat nearby. After two long whistles, the train began to move.

Shortly after retiring from the Navy, Ryan had landed a job as a security officer at a large industrial complex in Seattle. He'd planned to use the income from that, plus his military retirement, to keep Shelby afloat while the diner was closed.

He hadn't needed to. The diner's business-interruption coverage had reimbursed her loss of income. Fortunately, Shelby and Chloe had been able to occupy the apartment not long after the fire. Four weeks ago, the contractor had completed the repairs on the diner, and business had been booming ever since.

As the train chugged toward the Snoqualmie River Valley, a breeze blew into the car, whipping Shelby's hair into her face. But the June air was comfortable, the sun shining from a sparsely clouded sky.

Shelby stared out the wide opening, quieter than usual. Late last night, he'd picked up her and Chloe at the Seattle airport, where they'd arrived after visiting Arizona. The trip had been brief, but emotionally draining.

He reached over the arms of their chairs and took Shelby's hand. "You okay?"

"Yeah. At least, I will be." She turned to face him. "I guess I had unrealistic expectations. I thought our visit would make a difference for my mom, that getting to hold her only grandchild would draw her out of herself and into the world around her."

Ryan nodded. Mia had made the trip when Chloe was a baby, and Shelby had brought Chloe to Mia's funeral, so this wasn't the only time Mrs. Adair had seen her grandchild. But it had been Shelby's first opportunity to visit since her aunt's health failed.

She dropped her gaze to her lap. "Most of the time, my mom didn't seem to know Chloe was there. And I felt like an imposter, a poor substitute for the daughter they really wanted to see."

Ryan's heart twisted at the pain behind her words. "Sometimes people are so focused on what they've lost they can't see the blessings right in front of them."

And that was what Shelby was—a blessing—and he'd thanked God again and again for bringing them together. He planned to spend the rest of his life reminding her of just how amazing she was.

She lifted her gaze and gave him a sad smile. "I've never been able to help *my* mom, but maybe I can help Rachel's."

He squeezed her hand. "You already have."

Not only was she making sure his stepmother got to spend quality time with Chloe on a regular basis, but she'd also encouraged Ryan to become part of her life. In the months since his father's arrest, Ryan had bonded with her more than he ever had as a child. Now dinners together were weekly events.

The train drew to a stop. A steep upward slope formed a brush-covered wall on one side. On the other, the Snoqualmie Valley spread out before them. Beyond the chain-link fence bordering the track, the ground dropped off sharply. Farther down, the Snoqualmie River was a wide ribbon of blue and white through a rolling blanket of evergreens.

Shelby rose to take pictures, and Chloe slid from Ryan's lap to join her. As he watched them standing side by side, Chloe clutching the board that formed a handrail across the opening, his heart swelled. The two girls he loved more than anyone in the world.

He dropped his gaze to the backpack at his feet. The main zippered pouch held their lunch, along with some bottles of water. After leaving the scenic view, they would make a quick stop at the hydroelectric museum, then get off the train for a picnic in Snoqualmie Park.

Some time later, they approached the depot. As the train slowed, Ryan's pulse raced. Lunch wasn't all he had planned for the park. The smaller zippered compartment in his pack held a little hinged box.

Three months ago, he and Shelby had agreed to take it slow. It was what they'd both needed. In recent weeks, he'd prayed long and hard, and he was ready to take the next step. Unless he'd read her incorrectly, Shelby might be, too.

When the train came to a stop, Chloe slid from his lap and patted his pack. "Eat."

He slid his arms through the straps and

hoisted it onto his back. "That's right. We're going to have a picnic."

They crossed the small street that ran beside the depot and headed past a rose garden. A white gazebo stood in front of them, pavers circling it, leading visitors into the rest of the park.

"House." Chloe pointed and pulled them toward the two brick steps. A picnic table occupied one side of the octagon-shaped structure, a bench the other.

"You want to eat inside the gazebo?"

The answer was an excited squeal. She climbed onto the seat, and Ryan and Shelby took their places on either side of her. Nearby, the train released two long whistles and started to move away. In two hours, it would be back to take them to the North Bend depot, where Ryan had left his vehicle.

Chloe pointed at the pack. "Sammich."

"What do you say?" Shelby's tone was gentle.

"Peez."

Ryan reached inside. "Yes, you can have a sandwich."

He'd made three of them that morning, peanut butter and jelly. Then he'd washed some apples and packed a paring knife and a bag of chips. It wasn't gourmet fare, but it fit in his pack and didn't have to be kept cool.

After he'd blessed their food, both Chloe and Shelby tackled their lunch with enthusiasm, but each bite he took seemed to stick in his throat.

What if he was rushing things? What if Shelby wasn't ready? Maybe this wasn't the right setting. Maybe he should get a babysitter, take Shelby to a nice restaurant and propose by candlelight.

No, he knew Shelby better than that. Nothing relaxed or inspired her more than being in nature, enjoying God's creation.

And he didn't need to arrange a babysitter. This little girl they both loved was the sole reason they'd been brought together.

As he worked on chewing the last stubborn bite of his sandwich, he let his gaze shift to the side. A large flagpole rose from the center of the park, trees planted in a circle around the curved walkway. He inhaled deeply, drawing in the tranquility of their surroundings.

When he looked back at Shelby, she'd just finished slicing an apple and was handing pieces to Chloe. He cleared his throat. "I've been doing some thinking."

Her gaze snapped to his face. She'd probably heard the tightness in his tone. Was that uneasiness he saw, or was she just waiting for him to continue? His heart beat harder.

He blurted out the words before he could

change his mind. "I think Chloe needs a mom and dad instead of an aunt and uncle. We've been bouncing her between my apartment and yours for the past three months." He forced a smile. "She's probably wondering where home is."

Shelby lifted her brows. "Are you saying we should get married?"

His heart skipped a beat. Was she really going to make it that easy?

She put a hand over his, which was resting on the table. "I appreciate you being willing to make the sacrifice, but thousands of children grow up in broken homes, shuttled between mother and father, and turn out just fine."

*Sacrifice?* So much for being romantic. He was messing this up badly.

He moved to sit at Shelby's other side, then slid the knife from her fingers. While their niece munched on apple slices, he took both of Shelby's hands in his.

"That came out wrong." He should have planned what he would say. He didn't remember how he'd done it the first time. In fact, three months with Shelby had erased much of the time he'd spent with his ex-wife and the damage it had done to his psyche.

He squeezed her hands. "I love you, Shelby,

and I want you to be my wife. Not for Chloe's sake, but for mine. And I hope for yours."

Her gaze fluttered to the table as indecision skittered across her face. He knew how she felt about him. They'd both professed their love numerous times. Could he convince her to set aside her fears and trust him?

"Please don't be afraid. I promise I'll never belittle or try to control you. I want you to see yourself the way I see you, and the way God sees you—beautiful and intelligent."

Her lips lifted in a shaky smile. "You've helped me catch glimpses."

He squeezed her hands, waiting for the word he hoped to hear.

She moistened her lips. "I trust you, in a way I never thought possible."

*And?*

"I know what it's taken for you to get to this point, and I promise I'll never even look at another man. I love you, Ryan McConnell. You and only you."

His heart bobbed around in his chest, pounding out an erratic rhythm. "Does this mean you'll marry me?"

"Yes, I'll marry you."

He pulled her to her feet, lifted her over the bench and spun her around. After setting her down in the center of the gazebo, he drew her into his embrace. Chloe looked at them over one shoulder, an apple slice in her hand. About twenty yards away, a family sat at one of the picnic tables.

But Ryan didn't care who was watching. He lowered his mouth to hers and experienced the same jolt he always did, that same sense of wonder. He'd never get tired of kissing this woman, of holding her and loving her. She was the fulfillment of every dream he'd ever had.

And one dream in particular.

He'd entertained it for a brief moment, back in his apartment—that desire to have a family of his own. Then he'd dismissed it, sure it was out of his reach.

He'd been wrong. He was going to have that longed-for family—a beautiful, faithful wife and an adorable little girl.

God had granted him the desires of his heart.

* * * * *

Dear Reader,

I hope you've enjoyed Ryan and Shelby's story and beautiful North Bend, Washington. Earlier this year, my sister and I visited friends there. I was quite taken with the town and so inspired by all the amazing scenery. I decided it would be a great setting for a story. Apparently I'm not the only one, since the TV series *Twin Peaks* was also filmed there.

Both Ryan and Shelby grew up in dysfunctional homes, but they each had someone with a strong faith who was a guiding light. For Ryan, it was his best friend's father. For Shelby, it was her aunt. And though the path was winding and it took some time for both of them to come to the place of developing their own faith, eventually those long-ago efforts bore fruit.

May we each be that "someone" whom God uses to make an eternal impact on others' lives.

Love in Christ,
*Carol*

# Get 4 FREE REWARDS!

## We'll send you 2 FREE Books plus 2 FREE Mystery Gifts.

**Love Inspired®** books feature contemporary inspirational romances with Christian characters facing the challenges of life and love.

FREE Value Over $20

---

# Get 4 FREE REWARDS!

## We'll send you 2 FREE Books plus 2 FREE Mystery Gifts.

**Harlequin® Heartwarming™ Larger-Print** books feature traditional values of home, family, community and—most of all—love.

FREE
Value Over
$20

# THE FORTUNES OF TEXAS COLLECTION!

**18 FREE BOOKS in all!**

**Treat yourself to the rich legacy of the Fortune and Mendoza clans in this remarkable 50-book collection. This collection is packed with cowboys, tycoons and Texas-sized romances!**

**YES!** Please send me **The Fortunes of Texas Collection** in Larger Print. This collection begins with 3 FREE books and 2 FREE gifts in the first shipment. Along with my 3 free books, I'll also get the next 4 books from The Fortunes of Texas Collection, in LARGER PRINT, which I may either return and owe nothing, or keep for the low price of $5.24 U.S./$5.89 CDN each plus $2.99 for shipping and handling per shipment*. If I decide to continue, about once a month for 8 months I will get 6 or 7 more books but will only need to pay for 4. That means 2 or 3 books in every shipment will be FREE! If I decide to keep the entire collection, I'll have paid for only 32 books because 18 books are FREE! I understand that accepting the 3 free books and gifts places me under no obligation to buy anything. I can always return a shipment and cancel at any time. My free books and gifts are mine to keep no matter what I decide.

☐ 269 HCN 4622          ☐ 469 HCN 4622

Name (please print)

Address                                                                 Apt. #

City                              State/Province                 Zip/Postal Code

### Mail to the **Reader Service:**
**IN U.S.A.:** P.O. Box 1341, Buffalo, N.Y. 14240-8531
**IN CANADA:** P.O. Box 603, Fort Erie, Ontario L2A 5X3